JOURNEY
of the
HEART

JOURNEY
of the
HEART

The Lewis and Clark Expedition
Through the Eyes of
Sacagawea and Captain William Clark

CHARLOTTE ELLINGTON

Cover art: Insert pictures—Lewis and Clark at Three Forks, E.S. Paxton, 1912, courtesy of Montana Historical Society, X1912.07.01

Background cover photo by Ivana Cajina on Unsplash. Horse and compass illustrations by Freepik.

Published in the United States by Charlotte Ellington, St. Louis, Missouri

First Edition

ISBN 978-0-578-60387-2

For Ed

Dear Reader,

Thank you for your interest in *Journey of the Heart: The Lewis and Clark Expedition Through the Eyes of Sacagawea and Captain William Clark.*

When I first began this project, I only intended to write a brief account of Sacagawea's life to be included with other stories of Native American women. But as I began to research, I became so captivated with the story that I couldn't rest until I had taken in as much information as I felt was out there. I read numerous books and various sections of the Lewis and Clark diaries. I traveled to sites in St. Louis and St. Charles, Missouri, and Yellowstone, Wyoming. I visited and spoke with women of the Shoshone tribe near the Wind River Reservation. At every turn, I found myself more and more fascinated with this amazing story, which so beautifully represents the spirit and zeal of American adventure and enterprise, while also serving as a window into the life of many Native American tribes.

My goal as a writer was to capture the experience of the expedition with a simple, direct style that remained true to the actual facts. In addition, I strove to illuminate the remarkable characters of both William Clark and Sacagawea. Above all, I wanted to create a work that would leave readers feeling as if they themselves had participated in this grand and epic voyage.

I sincerely hope that your reading of the novel will be as rewarding and inspiring for you as the actual writing of the book was for me.

A special thank you to my husband Ed and to the members of the Creative Writing Workshop at the Daniel Boone Library in Ellisville, Missouri. Their enthusiasm and constructive comments spurred me onward. Thanks also to my good friends, Carole and Vic Heisserer, who loaned (?) me their copy of *Undaunted Courage* by Stephen Ambrose. That book was a cherished and frequently consulted companion during my writing.

Sincerely,

Charlotte Ellington

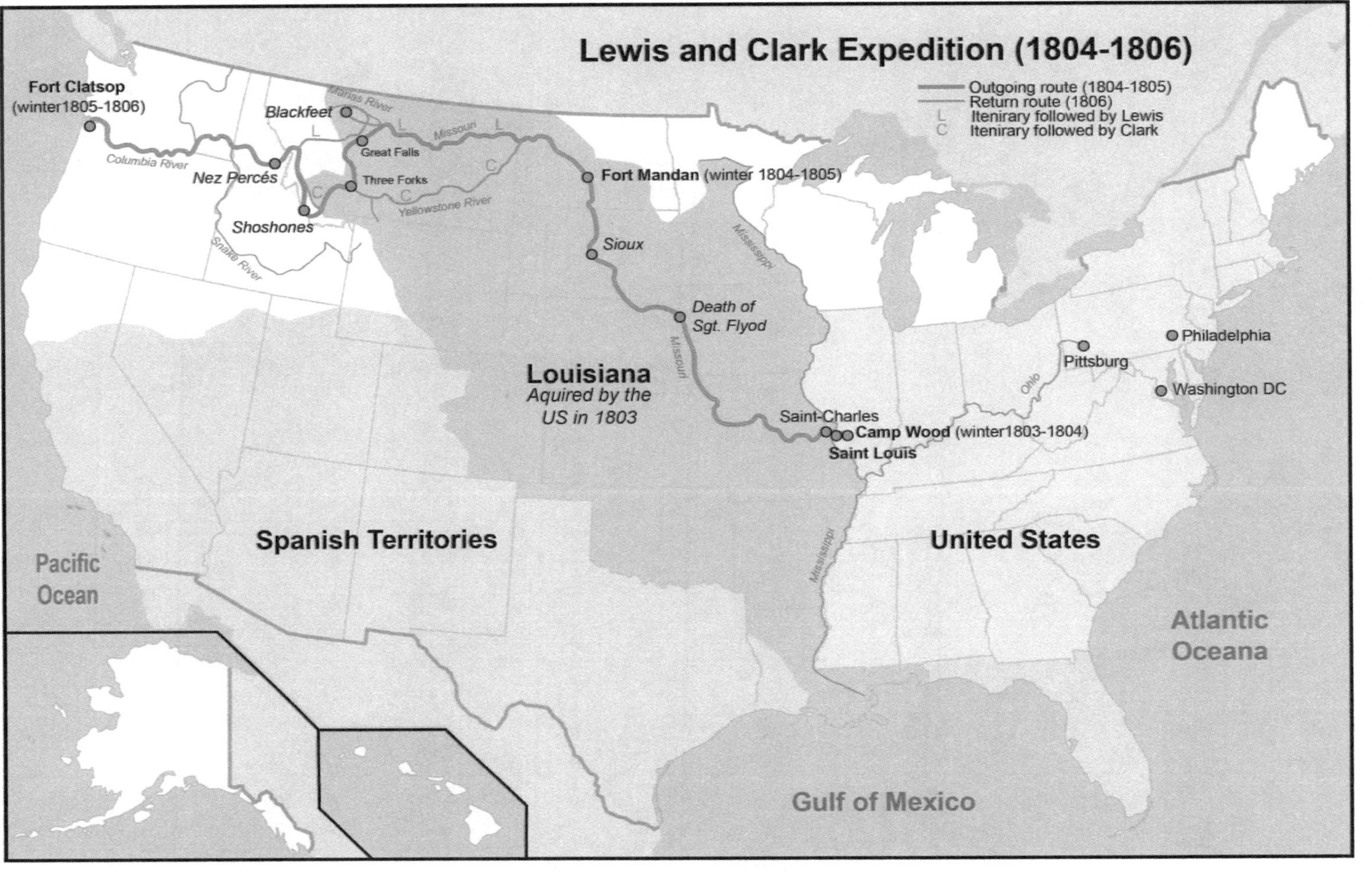

Lewis and Clark Expedition (1804-1806)
Outgoing route (1804-1805)
Return route (1806)
L   Itenirary followed by Lewis
C   Itenirary followed by Clark
Fort Clatsop
(winter1805-1806)
Blackfeet
Marias River
Columbia River
Great Falls
Missouri
Nez Percés
Three Forks
Yellowstone River
Shoshones
Snake River
Fort Mandan (winter 1804-1805)
Sioux
Mississippi
Death of
Sgt. Flyod
Missouri
Louisiana
Aquired by the
US in 1803
Philadelphia
Pittsburg
Ohio
Washington DC
Saint-Charles
Camp Wood (winter1803-1804)
Saint Louis
Spanish Territories
United States
Pacific
Ocean
Mississippi
Atlantic
Oceana
Gulf of Mexico

TABLE OF CONTENTS

1788–1804
IDAHO TO NORTH DAKOTA

SACAGAWEA

My life had already been one of many twists and turns
when I first met Captain Clark,
whom the native peoples call Chief Red Hair.
I wanted to travel with his tribe of men
on the journey over the mountains
to the Big Lake where water and sky meet.
But when I looked into his eyes that day in the Mandan-Hidatsa village,
I saw immediately the many doubts and questions.

Still, he was persuaded,
by his own thoughts, I judged, rather than our speech.
He did not know at that time
that our journey together would be such a long one,
or that it would be a journey of the heart
as well as a journey across land.
Nor did I.

I am called Sacagawea, Bird Woman.
The mothers in the village told me that as a small child,

I hopped from one spot to the next
in imitation of my bird friends,
and that is how I acquired my name.

As a young girl I lived with my family—
my sister, my brother, my father, and my mother—
in a village high in the mountains near the River of Salmon.
My days were busy.
From an early age, I helped with cooking, drying meat,
preparing furs, tanning leather, making blankets,
weaving baskets, and caring for the children.

When I was but a child of five,
my life was promised to an older man.
My husband-to-be presented my family with two horses and a mule.
My father agreed that the marriage would take place
the year I turned fourteen.

My people were the Shoshone, the valley dwellers.
We once lived in rich valleys where buffalo roamed—
a land with streams of gentle flowing water
and plains of high grasses.

We had fine horses of various colors:
pale like the sand of the river beaches,
brown like the bark of a tree,
black like the night sky,
gray like the smoke rising from fire.
Sometimes the colors were mixed together
so that our horses were spotted, dappled, ribboned, and flecked.

These horses had been acquired in generations past
from the Comanche people who lived to the south.
The Comanche had first traded for the horses
with the Spanish conquistadors of Mexico.

For a hundred years my people bred and trained fine horses,
producing a remarkable line of steeds
who ran with swift, sure feet
amongst enemy arrows or stampeding buffalo.
Warriors from many tribes
traveled long distances to barter for our horses.

When I was a young girl, I often stole visits
to the corrals where the horses rested.
I fed them apple roots and let them nuzzle my warm hands.
Stroking their necks, I praised their beauty and courage,
and I dreamed of a day when I would ride one of them across the prairie.
It was an unlikely dream, I knew,
for a Shoshone woman's task was to tend the pack horses,
while the Shoshone men trained horses for the plains.

Still, one fall evening,
when the sun had slipped behind the mountains,
and the ghost of a moon appeared in the sky,
I spoke in a coaxing voice to the red Appaloosa.
I threw one leg gently over her back,
pulled myself to a straddling position,
and pressed my knee against her flank.
We galloped across the prairie,
the tufts of grass rolling beneath us,
our hair flying in the wind.
We stopped when we reached
the foothills of the mountain
and returned at a slower canter,
our breath coming in deep gulps.

Of course, my brother was there to greet me,
but he said nothing in reproach,
simply guiding the horse back into the corral.

Yes, my people were good with horses,
but we were not so good with war,
for we did not have guns.
Even our swiftest horses could not outrun
the speeding fire that came from the rifle.
So we were pushed out of the valley
and forced to retreat high into the mountains,
where we lived on roots and berries.
For meat we ate fish, deer, rabbit, and sometimes antelope.
Our days were filled with hard work;
our nights were long and cold;
our stomachs cried with hunger pangs.

After several years, we determined
that we could not live without the buffalo.
We yearned for the rich, dark meat—
a meat that could be hung and dried
so that it lasted for a full year.
We needed buffalo skin and hide
to make our tents and sleeping robes.
We needed buffalo bones
to make utensils for cooking and eating.

We waited until the time when the buffalo were fattest,
when they had feasted for several moons on lush, green grasses.
Then we took down our teepees,
loaded our possessions on our travois,
and descended the mountain
to the place where the three rivers come together.
We posted our guards close to the camp
and sent our scouts to the higher places to keep lookout.
Always we kept our eyes and ears alert,
for we had many enemies
who did not wish to share the buffalo.

When we judged the conditions safe,
four of our men and three of our women
sang the song to call in the buffalo.
Our shaman danced before the fire for an entire evening.
In the morning, he declared our intention for a successful hunt
and informed the hunters where they might find the buffalo.

It was a good year for killing buffalo—
the year that I was eleven.
Our hunters spent long days stalking and hunting,
bringing many huge beasts to the ground.
Our women worked hard, butchering and preparing meat.
We rejoiced and feasted on tasty beef and buffalo fat.

On our last day, we began packing our belongings.
The mothers sent us older children
to the banks of the stream in search of sweet berries.
My friends and I laughed as we danced across the meadow.
Alongside us, bright yellow flowers
with deep brown eyes swayed in the breeze.
We looked forward to one last evening of feasting and games.
The sound of the rushing stream was a welcome one.
I pointed to a patch of purple berries across the water.
But before we reached the river bank,
I felt thunder in the ground,
and I knew it was not the thunder of buffalo.

I stopped and looked behind me.
Jumping Fish, my friend, grabbed my arm.
We stood frozen for a moment as the thunder grew,
and then we knew.
"Run!" I cried, pulling Jumping Fish's hand.
I pointed to an island, across the shallow water.
If we could make it there,
we could hide under the low-hanging branches.

But we had only stepped a few feet into the shallow water
when the thunder was upon us.
As I turned, I saw the savage faces painted black,
descending from the horses.
Brutal arms closed around me.
I felt myself lifted.
Pain tore through my chest, and breath left my body
as my legs arced through the air.
I was bound with leather thongs
and planted behind my captor on his horse.
His painted steed galloped forward and then circled back.
My eyes met those of Jumping Fish, who was likewise bound.
There was no surprise on her face,
and I judged there was none on mine.
We were captured.

Still, my eyes darted about,
while my mind wildly searched for a way to escape.
But as I looked to the village, I saw rising smoke.
As the horse galloped closer, my horror grew,
for the leaping flames were devouring our tents.
I turned my face and lowered my eyes.
I did not want to think about my kinsmen.
A young girl is a prized catch, valued for her work, but the others?
The mothers and small children would be too much trouble for travel,
and the young braves too much of a risk.
They would rather fight and die than be a captive.
So why would they be spared?

We rode for many days, and always
I looked for chances to break free,
but I remained bound with thongs,
whether I was on the horse
or tethered to a pole on the ground.
When I squirmed or whimpered,
I was threatened with knives and spears.

I learned to keep my thoughts quiet.
I learned to keep my body still.

We traveled over mountains and through swampy marshes.
The horses wound their way along narrow paths through thick forests.
On some days, the sun was on our backs;
on other days, we were pelted with rain.
If my captors were in a good mood,
I was fed scraps of meat.
Sometimes I was not fed at all.

When I smelled cooking fires,
I knew we were close to the home of these warriors.
When the village came into view,
I marveled at its vastness,
for stretched out as far as my eye could see
were the lodges of these people.
They did not live in teepees.
No, their homes were rounded, wooden domes with roofs.
These dwellings were so large
that even the horses and dogs could be brought inside at night.
The people slept on raised beds covered with deerskins and blankets.

Their food was much different than the food of my people,
for although they dug for roots,
they also cultivated gardens where they grew crops: corn, beans, squash.
The meat of these crops was sweet and rich.
I had never tasted such food before.
These people even had plots of land
to grow the tobacco for their smoking ceremonies.

In this place, I first saw white men.
Several of them lived in the villages with native wives.
Their skin was pale like a fading moon.
Hair grew beneath their noses and also on their cheeks.
They often wore clothes of deer or antelope skin like native peoples,

but their clothes fit closely to their bodies.
They wore hats of beaver or fox fur.

I found the life of a captive squaw a brutal one,
with much grueling work and no kind words.
The language was different from my own,
and I struggled for many months before I could converse.

I was not allowed to roam freely
or to travel to the stream with the other girls my age.
I was confined to the watch of my new Hidatsa family.
When I was finally allowed to accompany other women
in search of berries and roots,
my eyes carefully searched the face of every young girl.
I hoped to find Jumping Fish,
but never did I see her.
I reasoned that she had been traded to the Mandan people,
who lived on the opposite side of the village.

In the daytime, my mind was occupied with many tasks.
In the evenings, however, when I lay upon my bed,
I thought of my Shoshone family—
of my sister, who could run a foot race faster than any of the braves;
of my brother, who rode a horse and shot straight arrows;
of my mother, who painted buffalo blankets;
of my father, who loved to sit with the other men,
smoking tobacco from the long pipe.
On those evenings, I vowed I would return to my Shoshone home.

Still, in the time in between, I worked hard.
I dug roots and harvested vegetables.
I prepared hides and sewed new garments.
I performed small kindnesses for the mothers and grandmothers.
My work was rewarded,
for after I had been there for three summers,
I was adopted into the tribe.

In a special ceremony, the mothers presented me
with my own digging stick.
The handle had been carefully fashioned of bone;
the point had been slowly charred and oiled.
I was also presented with a belt of blue beads,
the gift of highest honor,
for blue beads are the most precious of all beads,
given as a token of gratitude to only a chosen few.

Perhaps it was the blue beads
that first caught the eye of the white man, Charbonneau.
I often saw him looking at me.
He already had a young wife and a small child,
but he must have felt he needed another.
One morning my adoptive father told me
that I would now live with this man.
Charbonneau's "other" wife, Otter Woman,
informed me that I had been won in a game of chance.

I did not think it a bad thing.
I knew Charbonneau was not a young man,
for the hair that grew on his head and face
was dark in some places and white in others.
He would not be like the younger braves
who yearned for the life of war and games.
No, he was a man of years,
a respected tradesman,
who could provide well for two wives.
Besides, Otter Woman was a Shoshone captive like me.
She had been taken from a different tribe than my own;
we had not known each other in other times.
Still, it was good to be with someone
close to my own age, from my own people.
In the evening, when Charbonneau smoked with the men,
we laughed and shared stories of our early life.

We were never hungry in those days.
Charbonneau always provided fresh meat,
and unlike the native hunters,
Charbonneau was a fine cook,
who made sausages and soups and meats with rich sauces.

Charbonneau's work of trapping animals and selling fur
often required travel to other villages and to trading posts.
I enjoyed these travels where we met with new people.
I especially loved to see the trading villages,
where the white men lived and gathered.

Like the Hidatsa braves, however,
Charbonneau could be a harsh husband.
He sometimes struck me when he judged I was not hurrying enough,
or if a task did not meet his satisfaction,
or if he himself failed at a task—
like the time his string of pelts
was left behind when the tying thong broke.
He swore at me then and delivered a blow
that knocked me to the ground.

I knew that Charbonneau was content in his work
but not so content in his life.
Like me, he was living with a people who were not his own.
Sometimes Otter Woman and I asked him about his other life.
He described the square houses made of smooth wood
in the village of Montreal, where his people lived.
These houses were sturdy and could last for years.
He told us about the sacred lodges with pointed roofs
where the people sang praises,
and the holy men told stories of the white man's god.
We asked him about his kinsmen,
but he would not speak about
his father and mother or sisters and brothers.

Spring 1803–Fall 1804
MISSOURI TO NORTH DAKOTA

CLARK

When I first saw the young Indian squaw,
I was frankly filled with misgivings.
I saw the necessity of including her,
for we would definitely need to acquire horses
if we were to cross the mountains,
and we were told her people, the Shoshone,
were the ones to supply them.
Still . . . she looked so young.
And in her condition?
How could we not think of her as a hindrance?

Captain Lewis and I spent considerable time
that day discussing the probabilities.
We agreed to sleep on the matter before we made a decision.
Sleep eluded me that evening, however,
and I found myself reviewing our progress thus far.

Our great adventure began in the spring of 1803
when my friend and comrade, Meriwether Lewis,

invited me to share the commission
assigned to him by President Jefferson.
He was to lead an expedition to explore the land
recently acquired by the United States from Napoleon of France.
The Louisiana Purchase was a vast tract of land,
lying west of the Mississippi,
with waterways leading to the Pacific Ocean.

My heart leapt at the opportunity.
I quickly responded that such an enterprise
was one that I had longed for.
I assured him that I fully realized
the difficulties we would encounter,
and I declared that I would prefer the company
of no other man than himself—Meriwether Lewis—
in this grand endeavor.

The Corps of Discovery was our official title.
Jefferson outlined our mission clearly.
Our first and foremost task was to explore the Missouri River,
mapping the waters and tributaries that would
provide a direct passageway to the Pacific Ocean.
Establishing this route would do much
to ensure our nation's dominance
in fur trading and other areas of commerce.

Secondly, we were to acquaint ourselves
with the various Indian tribes along our route.
We were to treat them in the utmost "friendly and conciliatory manner,"
informing them of our peaceable intentions,
allaying any fears or ill feelings,
and assuring them of our continued patronage,
while also making them aware of our sovereign power.

And thirdly, but of no less importance,
we were to keep accurate journals,

reflecting the customs and habits of the native peoples
and describing the plant life, the animals, the terrain, the waterways.
I, having some experience as a cartographer,
was charged with the task of mapping the new lands.
Lewis, for his part, would write detailed descriptions,
make sketches, and collect appropriate samples.
We were well aware that this land
represented a vast, rich, unexplored expansion
of our country's natural boundaries.

We began our preparations in July of 1803
with the building of our keelboat,
a vessel fifty-five feet in length and eight feet wide.
Propelled by twenty-two oars and a square sail,
it had the capacity to carry ten to twelve tons of goods and supplies.
Twenty-two storage lockers formed a catwalk,
which our crew could walk upon to pole the keelboat at various points.
When opened, the locker tops formed a breastwork
along the gunwales for protection from attack.

In addition, we constructed two pirogues—
flat-bottomed open boats, equipped with a sail.
Each held a blunderbuss, which could fire shot with a scattering effect.
Our white pirogue had six oars and was manned by six military soldiers.
The red one was operated by a party of French boatmen.

We spent considerable time selecting our corps.
We needed soldiers, hunters, cooks, woodsmen,
interpreters, blacksmiths, gunsmiths, carpenters, and boatmen.
We searched for men of strong character,
who demonstrated self-reliance, physical strength, and endurance—
men who were independent but knew how to take orders.

After several months of interviews and scrutiny,
we were satisfied with our selected crew,
which consisted of nine woodsmen from Kentucky,

fourteen soldiers with the United States Army, eleven French watermen,
three sergeants, one interpreter, and two captains—myself and Lewis.
My man, York, who had been with me since childhood,
was also enlisted as well as Lewis's Newfoundland dog, Seaman.

THE RIVER, THE LAND, THE WILDLIFE

Our official departure from St. Louis was made on May 16, 1804.
Several days into our voyage, we stopped at a large cave
known to French traders as Tavern Rock.
Travelers often camp at this location,
and both Indian and white men have left carvings
and writings on the limestone walls.
Captain Lewis was determined to scale the walls of the cliff
to survey the land and the river from the highest vantage point.
He was nearly atop the 300-foot bluff
when he lost his footing and began sliding.
With only twenty feet to spare, his knife caught in a crevice,
and he was saved from what surely would have been
a disastrous death and an early termination of our mission.

Navigation of the river in those early days
was far more difficult than we had expected.
We struggled mightily against the strong currents on the Missouri.
Eroding banks collapsed at frequent intervals,
dumping trees, roots, mud, and debris into the waters.
Concealed logs and limbs often floated just below the surface.
I frequently abandoned the ride and walked along the shore
to better alert the crew to impediments.
We used long cords of rope to pull the vessels through shallow waters.
It was a slow and laborious process;
sometimes we only traveled a few miles a day.

The ever-changing scenery was a constant source of wonderment.
In the early days, the terrain was similar to that which we knew—
hardwood trees and familiar flowers flourished along the river banks.

As the treed banks faded,
a starker landscape appeared—
one of tall, majestic, limestone bluffs.
September brought us to a completely new terrain
where long stretches of prairie grasses rippled in the breeze.

The wildlife we encountered provided us with both
a source of amusement and a sense of awe.
We noted species and variations
completely unknown to us in the East.

Coyote

Of special interest was a type of prairie wolf
about the size of a gray fox.
He had a bushy tail and the head and ears of a wolf.
Rarely found alone, these creatures hunted in packs.
Their noisy barking was similar to that of a small cur dog.

Prairie Dog

Captain Lewis and I came upon another unusual species of "dog"
one evening while out for a pleasant stroll on the prairie.
Suddenly, we realized we were surrounded by
small, squirrel-like creatures who popped their heads
out of the ground at regular intervals
while making the most curious, whistling noise.
Exiting their burrows, they would sit on their hind legs
and chatter back and forth.
Our interpreters tell us they are called *le petit chien,*
or *small dog,* by the French.
Entire villages of these animals live in burrows on the prairie.
We spent nearly a full day attempting to unearth one.
We finally triumphed by pouring barrels of water down the holes,
thereby flushing our specimen from his home.
We nabbed him before he could execute an escape.

Buffalo

In August we spotted a conic-shaped hill
that the Oto Indians had warned us about.
They insisted the site was inhabited by a tribe of devils,
who appeared human in some ways,
but who possessed remarkably large heads.
These devils stood a mere eighteen inches high.
Well-armed with sharp arrows,
they could easily shoot from a great distance.
Always watchful, they would readily kill any person
who attempted to approach their hill.

We thought the report worth investigating.
When we breached the top of the hill,
we saw no devils, but we were rewarded
with a sweeping, panoramic view of the plains
where thousands of buffalo grazed.
We marveled at these great, shaggy creatures
with their heavy, thick coats and their peculiar, humped backs.

Pronghorns

Another curious creature was the buck goat.
This animal is about the height of a deer, with a shorter body.
He has a pair of hooves on each foot.
His nostrils are large, but his eyes are sheep like.
I think he is more similar to the antelope,
or perhaps the gazelle of Africa,
than he is to an actual goat.

Jackrabbit

We encountered hares of considerable size and speed.
It was not easy getting a shot at them,
for they traveled alone and were quick.
I judged that any one of them could easily outrun the fastest horse.
Captain Lewis measured the length of one specimen's leaps

and found it to be an astonishing twenty-one feet.

Pelicans

One of our most unusual encounters
with a bird species occurred in August.
I was riding in the cabin of our keelboat
when one of the bowmen called to me,
for a blanket of white was coming down the river.
Hurrying to the bow, I stared down into the water.
As the white blanket engulfed us, I realized
we were looking upon a sea of white feathers—
three miles long, seventy yards wide.
When we rounded the bend, we discovered the source,
for there was a large sandbar covered with white pelicans.
In the midst of their summer molt,
they were preening themselves.
The flock stretched over several acres of land.
The mosquitoes were so thick, unfortunately,
I could not take aim,
so I shot into the thick of them,
bringing a specimen in to examine.
We could not believe the size of his pouch.
When we poured water into it, we found that it held five gallons.

Grizzly

Pierre Cruzatte, our interpreter and fiddler,
was the first to get a shot at a grizzly.
I had seen his footprint the day before
and declared it the largest bear print I had ever seen.
All of the men were curious and anxious to get a look,
but Cruzatte was so awed by the bear's size and formidable appearance
that he managed only one shot
then dropped his tomahawk and gun and retreated.

OUR CREW

We were largely impressed with the service
of our men in these early days.
Toiling in the summer heat,
they were continuously plagued by mosquitoes and gnats.
They suffered greatly from dysentery,
which I believed to be caused by the brackish water.
The boils and tumors, which erupted on their skin,
were equally distressing.
Lewis had brought a considerable stock of medicines,
and he liberally dispensed various preparations.

Sergeant Charles Floyd failed to respond to our treatments.
For a number of days, he lay in agony
with a painful stomach ailment.
One evening he informed me that he would be going away.
He asked that I write a letter
to be delivered to his parents.
He died with great composure.
We buried him with military honors
on top of a bluff, which we named Floyd's Bluff.
We also gave his name to the branch of the river that flowed beneath.
The men lamented his death.
Captain Lewis and I were likewise saddened,
for he had given us constant proof
of his determined resolution to serve his country well.

Unfortunately, we were required
to take disciplinary action upon several occasions.
Captain Willard was caught sleeping at his post.
He pled guilty to the charge of lying down but denied falling asleep.
He was, nevertheless, convicted of both counts
and assigned the punishment of one hundred lashes.

Private Moses Reed deserted our party
on the pretense of retrieving a knife he had left behind.
It took Drouillard, our best tracker, ten days to locate him.
Reed admitted to deserting and stealing a rifle,
a shot pouch, powder, and balls.
His actions warranted death.
We, however, were softened by the manly way
he admitted to his crimes
and sentenced him to run the gauntlet four times.
He endured no less than five hundred lashes.
We stripped him of his rank and dismissed him from our services.

EARLY ENCOUNTERS WITH NATIVE TRIBES

Our early encounters with Indian tribes proved to be perilous.
On September 23, we came upon three teenaged boys of the Sioux tribe.
Drouillard communicated with them through sign language,
asking them to inform their chiefs that
we wished to speak with them in council.
The next morning, however, one of our hunters, John Colter,
informed us that Indians had stolen his horse.
When we subsequently happened upon five Indian braves,
we sternly told them that we had come as friends,
but we would fight for what was ours,
and unless our horse was returned,
we would not speak with any Teton Sioux on pleasant terms.

We then proceeded further upriver and set up camp.
By 11 a.m. several chiefs and a number of warriors
came in and presented us with gifts,
including a large quantity of buffalo meat.
We offered them portions of our pork.
Our talks soon broke down, however,
when we discovered that our interpreter, Cruzatte,
knew only a few words in the Sioux language,
not enough to adequately communicate our thoughts.

Aware of the unease arising,
Captain Lewis called for a display of strength,
with our troops marching in uniform
and performing military maneuvers.
I presented a medal, a red military coat,
and a cocked hat to Black Buffalo.
Two of the other chiefs received smaller medals.
The lesser chiefs responded by appearing greatly insulted.

We invited all the chiefs on deck,
where we treated them to a quarter glass of whiskey.
One of them grabbed the bottle from our hands
and indicated he would like more.
We endeavored to communicate that our talks had ended.
With some difficulty, we were able to get the group back ashore,
where they insisted they be given a canoe full of gifts.
They assured us they would not depart without one.
My patience could endure no longer.
I informed them that we were not squaws, but warriors.
I drew my sword and ordered all men to assume arms.
The swivel gun was loaded with sixteen musket balls,
and Lewis held the lighted taper over it.
The shore quickly filled with warriors,
their bows strung and pointing toward us.
The situation was eased when Chief Black Buffalo
motioned to his warriors to take leave.

The next day, however, Chief Black Buffalo returned to our camp.
He invited us to his village, insisting that
he wished to prove his hospitality and good intentions.
We felt we could not refuse the invitation.
With much ceremony, we were carried
on a decorated buffalo robe to the council lodge,
where seventy warriors sat in a circle.
Slabs of buffalo meat were spread before us.
We smoked and talked.

Although the communication was difficult,
we understood that the chiefs wished us to know
that they were a very poor nation, deserving of our pity.
I informed them that we wished them to be at peace
with their neighbors, the Omahas,
and also with other tribes in the region.
They must have thought me mad,
for we were immediately treated to the Sioux scalp dance,
which consisted of men and women in highly decorated dress
carrying pointed sticks with the scalps of Omaha Indians.
They danced with tambourines fashioned from deer and goat hooves.
Our men tossed presents of tobacco and beads.
One warrior, however, did not feel he had received sufficient gifts
and flew into a fit of rage, storming out of the dance line.

We did not sleep well that night,
especially as Cruzatte had received word from an Omaha friend
that the Sioux had all along intended to rob us.

Our departure the next evening was fraught with intrigue once again.
By some misfortune, our pirogue slammed broadside into the keelboat.
"All hands up! All hands up!" I cried.
The chiefs interpreted those cries as evidence of the Omaha attacking.
In less than ten minutes, the bank was lined
with two hundred warriors led by Black Buffalo.
Lewis feared they were posed to attack us
and quickly ordered our men to take up their rifles.
Fortunately, both sides soon enough realized the error.
Unfortunately, we lost our anchor because of the collision of the boats
and were forced to stay another evening.

The next day, when we attempted to depart,
Black Buffalo appeared and boarded our vessel.
Once again, the banks were lined with well-armed Tetons.
Black Buffalo insisted we stay one more day.
Several warriors grabbed our bowline.

"I only want some tobacco," he informed us—a mere trifle.
We knew the significance of such a gesture, however.
It would mean the Sioux held the right to exact a toll of white men.

I threw the braves a carrot of tobacco
but informed the chief that he should demonstrate his influence
by taking the rope from his men so that we might depart peacefully.
Black Buffalo finally acceded to my request.
When we had sailed some distance, I yelled back
that if the Sioux were determined to stop us or make war,
we were ready to defend ourselves.
We did not sleep well for many nights after that.
I shuddered to think of the consequences
had events climaxed to a different resolution.

Luckily, we passed the next several weeks in a period of calm.
We were able to enjoy the splendor of fall days—
cloudless, blue skies and grasses turning golden brown.
With cooler evenings, the mosquito population diminished,
and we took pleasure in peaceful reflection around the fire.

We noted that the animals of the plain—
the elk, the antelope, and the buffalo—
were gathering into herds, preparing to migrate to winter grounds.
Overhead, we witnessed flocks of honking, quacking geese,
descending the river on their southern flight.

On October 8, we passed a three-mile-long island,
near the mouth of the Grand River,
which was home to three villages of Arikara Indians.
We judged about two thousand Indians lived in these villages.
They prospered with crops of beans, corn, and squash.
Two white traders, Joseph Gravelines and Pierre-Antoine Tableau,
were in the area and helped us establish relations.
We made our usual presentation and speeches
and then passed out presents:

vermilion paint, pewter, looking glasses,
needles, broadcloth, beads, combs,
razors, scissors, knives, tomahawks.
We didn't want anyone else calling us stingy,
so we gave out more than we had given before.
We offered whiskey, but the Arikaras refused,
saying they were surprised that their white father
should present them with liquor, which would make them act like fools.

We visited several villages in the afternoon
where York, my black slave, was quite a sensation.
The Arikaras were astounded by his impressive size,
black skin, and coarse, curly hair.
They surmised that he was related to the buffalo
and thereby imbued with special medicine powers.
York, for his turn, enjoyed playing with the children,
chasing them between the lodges,
bellowing as if he were a wild beast.
Crow at Rest, one of the chiefs, petitioned us to make a peace
between his people and the Mandans, at whose village we would soon be.

Unfortunately, we were forced to give our attention
to a situation requiring disciplinary measures.
Private John Newman, a grumbler by nature,
had been unfavorably influenced by his comrade Moses Reed.
He was found guilty by a court of peers
of uttering repeated mutinous expressions.
He was sentenced to seventy-five lashes
and then discarded from our party.
We were astonished by the reaction of one of the Arikara chiefs,
who was so greatly alarmed by the lashing
that he cried out loudly in protest.
I explained the cause of the punishment,
but the chief declared that his nation
never whipped their own children.

With winter approaching, we were anxious
to proceed to the Mandan villages.
We knew from our contacts that this town
was actually a collection of five villages,
made up of both Mandan and Hidatsa people.
The villages were a crossroads for the trade industry
for both white and Indian peoples.
We hoped to establish good relations
and secure a suitable place where we might build our winter quarters.

PART 2—THE MANDAN VILLAGE

November 1804–April 1805
NORTH DAKOTA

SACAGAWEA

And then came the day when the tribe of white men
arrived in their canoes.
These men were not traders, I knew,
for they wore fitted coats and pants of cloth.
The captains' coats were deep blue,
with red around the neck
and white along the edges.
They had several hats—round ones with medals
and flat ones shaped like crescent moons.

The two captains of this tribe told us
they had been sent by the chief of the white nation.
Captain Clark was a large man,
taller than any man in our village.
The people of the villages stared at him
for his hair was red, like a burning fire.
Captain Lewis was tall also,
with hair the color of sand
and eyes blue like the sky of a summer day.

The captains spent evenings smoking and talk with our headmen.
They gave our chiefs round, gold medals
with carvings of the head of the great American chief
who lived in the East.
This chief was now our Great Chief,
and both the white men and the red men
would be children of the same family.
The Great White Father would see
that we always had hunting land
and that we would never be hungry.

The captains passed out beads and knives.
They promised that future traders
would come and bring even more gifts.
For the time being, they would rest here,
they informed our chiefs,
for they were on a long journey
in search of the Big Waters that lay
on the other side of the mountain.
But the days were growing short,
and soon the mountain passes would be covered with snow.
They would not travel until the land was green again.

So they built a small village with eight dwellings.
Their lodgings were made of logs that fit together.
These buildings were not round, but square with equal sides.
They continued to consult with our tribesmen
as they worked and hunted and smoked in the evenings,
for they were worried.
They had heard that to get to the Big Waters,
they must cross high mountains.
Thus far, their journey had been one of river travel,
but they would need horses when they reached the mountains.
Did our men know where they could get these horses?

When I heard about these talks,
I was filled with excitement.
I reminded Charbonneau that my first people,
the Shoshone, were the people of horses.
I was confident that I could still speak my mother tongue.
I could help these men trade for horses.
Charbonneau looked at me, surprise on his face,
for these thoughts had not traveled to his mind yet.
He nodded, and a slow smile spread across his face.

Over the next few days, he spoke his own thoughts.
Yes, he was anxious to go on a journey,
for he was not one to stay long in a single place.
It would be good to travel with other white men,
some of whom spoke French, his native tongue.
He could serve as interpreter, for he knew sign talk
and several native languages.
For himself, it would be good to explore new lands
for hunting and trade.
Best of all, he would be paid with the white man's money,
money which could buy many goods
that would make our life comfortable.
So he wasted no time making his way
to the lodging of the white chiefs.

When Charbonneau returned, he told me
to prepare myself for meeting with these white men.
I put on my finest dress of elk skin, my belt of blue beads,
and my fringed and beaded moccasins.
But when I was presented to Captain Clark and Captain Lewis,
I saw surprise and fear in their eyes.
I was but a young girl, they declared.
They pointed to my belt, which was cinched above my waist,
and then looked back at Charbonneau.
Yes, he acknowledged, holding up two fingers.
Our child would be born before two moons had passed.

I stepped forward then and smiled at these captains.
I presented them with a buffalo blanket, which I had made myself.
I made signs to them, indicating that I could travel on this journey.
I pointed to my stomach and then to my back
to show that my child could travel on my back.
I signed that I could walk to the land of the horses
and talk to the people there, for we spoke the same language.
I do not know if they understood everything I said,
but Charbonneau made words in French,
which the interpreter, Labiche, translated to the captains.

I did not try to communicate the words of my heart—
how I desperately longed to make this journey;
how I wanted to see the faces of my own people;
how I hoped that some from my family had survived the massacre;
how I wished to be reunited with them.

Captains Lewis and Captain Clark were persuaded by our talk.
They agreed that we would travel with their men.
Charbonneau would be paid for his services as interpreter
with the white man's trade goods and money.

All of this was decided at the Great Time of Celebration,
when the white man recalls the birth of the holy child.
That night the men gathered around the fire
and passed around bottles of brandy and whiskey.
Monsieur Cruzatte, the man with one eye,
made music by rubbing strings on his box with a magic stick.
The men danced and sang songs.

Then it was the coldest time of year.
Thick blankets of snow covered the ground.
The time for my child to be born came upon me.
It was not an easy time, and I found
that what the other wives and mothers said was true.
Native mothers have an easy time when giving birth to babies

who are born to men of our tribe.
The pain is light, and the baby is quick
and anxious to see his new life,
but it is not so if the baby is born to a white man.
No, then it is a long, painful, violent time.
And so it was with me.
My body shook with wild pain.
I screamed for a day and a night,
but still no baby came.
I thought I would surely die.
Charbonneau asked Captains Lewis and Clark
if there was not a remedy in the box
of medicines they carried with them.
Surely, they carried some potion that would induce
the birth of a baby born to a white man.

The captains had no such medicine,
but they consulted with Monsieur Jessaume,
a Frenchman in our village living with a Mandan wife.
He counseled them to break the rattles of a snake
into small pieces and mix them with water.
Captain Lewis did so and had me drink the mixture,
and then quickly my baby jumped forth.
He was a fine, healthy boy,
whom I scolded in a gentle voice for causing such pain.
Charbonneau declared his name to be Jean Baptiste,
in honor of the kinsman of the holy infant.
I called him Pomp, which means *firstborn* in my language.
In the weeks that followed,
Charbonneau and I fashioned a cradleboard,
which I would strap on my back,
to carry my son on our long journey.

But alas, it seemed that all the agreements
were not agreed upon.
When it came time for Charbonneau to make his mark

on the white men's papers to seal our contract,
there was much arguing.
No, Charbonneau assured the captains,
he would not serve guard duty.
Nor would he carry heavy loads or dig pits.
He, Charbonneau, was not a soldier in this army,
taking orders from the captains.
He would remain, as always, the chief of himself.
Furthermore, he insisted, he would keep
the game and furs he acquired
so that he could make a profit at the trading posts.

Charbonneau crossed his arms and stood
with his chin thrust forward,
but I could see the white captains
would not be talked to in this manner.
Their words spit from their mouths.

Charbonneau turned his back on the white captains,
and we quickly returned to our quarters.
I waited until the next day before I asked Charbonneau what was said.
"They called me a troublemaker," he angrily retorted.
"And also accused me of accepting bribes at the French trading posts
to keep the Americans from opening their own trade routes.
I will not pull boats and dig pits
and do the work of the common soldier,
nor will I be falsely accused or ordered about!
'I am content to live with the Hidatsa,' I assured them."

For three days we went about our business,
but our hearts pressed heavily upon us.
On the fourth day, I persuaded Charbonneau
to speak with the captains again
and to declare his desire to be a good man.
He did so by sending them words on paper.
When he met with the captains this time,

hands were clasped in friendship and promise.
Charbonneau would travel on this journey as interpreter.
He would receive the pay of twenty-five dollars per month,
much more than other soldiers.
We would eat and live in the same teepees
and huts as Captain Clark and Captain Lewis,
where we would have protection and good food.
Charbonneau agreed that he would work alongside everyone else,
and yes, he would obey orders.

That winter was the coldest winter that I could remember.
My people did not think that the meat would last until spring thaw,
so they informed the white chiefs
that they would call in the buffalo for one final hunt.
For three nights our dancers performed the buffalo dance,
and our singers sang the sacred chants
that called in the spirit of the buffalo.
Two days after the dance, the prairie was covered with buffalo.
Our braves rode out and killed enough buffalo to make a small feast.
We hung strips of buffalo meat to last for the remainder of the winter.
While we waited for warmer days,
Charbonneau continued to trap rabbits and beaver.

Finally, we saw cracks on the ice in the river.
These cracks grew, and water pooled on top of the ice.
When the ice was reduced to scattered, floating chunks,
the captains agreed that, yes, we could depart.

October 1804–April 1805
NORTH DAKOTA

CLARK

In late October, we experienced our first snowfall.
We were much relieved a few days later
to reach the Mandan villages.
Although we knew it would be a large settlement,
we were, nevertheless, surprised by what we saw before us.
The citizens lived in sophisticated lodge dwellings.
We judged the population to be over four thousand,
larger than our own city of St. Louis.
We arrived at trading time and found the villages
not only full of Hidatsa and Mandan,
but also Crow, Cheyenne, Kiowa, and Arapaho.
Additionally, there were many white traders—British, American, French.
We were impressed with the array of goods:
leathers, trade guns, produce, meats, furs, blankets,
painted buffalo hides, horses, musical instruments.
The atmosphere was one of merriment and good times.

We were fortunate to make the acquaintance of René Jessaume,
a trader who had been living with the Mandans some fifteen years.

He participated fully in the Mandan life with his wife and children.
He volunteered to move into our camp.
He would apprise us of the people in this settlement
and also provide translation when needed.
We were glad to accommodate his suggestion.

We spoke in council with several of the chiefs:
Big White, Black Cat, Little Raven.
Big White was a man of enormous girth and very light skin.
We acknowledged the principal chiefs with a gift of a flag,
a medal with the image of our president,
a uniform coat, a hat, and a feather.
To the lesser chiefs, we gave smaller medals.
Black Cat informed us that the lesser chiefs were disappointed,
so we presented them with an iron corn mill.
They were quite amazed at the speed with which it could grind corn
and counted this as their most treasured gift.
In return, they presented us with bushels of corn
and nearly 165 pounds of fine meat.

The Indians pointed out that the mountains were already
covered with snow at the higher elevations.
They were too steep and rugged for travel.
We would need to wait for spring to continue.
We were satisfied with our talks and felt quite comfortable,
so we set about building a proper fort.
We built eight log huts, with four rooms in each hut.
An eighteen-foot stockade with a gate enclosed the area.
We included a sentry post with a mounted swivel gun.
The Indians came by daily as we worked,
observing our progress and offering advice.

In early November, we were visited
by the French Canadian, Toussaint Charbonneau.
I judged him to be about forty-five years of age.
He lived in the village with his two Shoshone squaws.

They were young women, he informed me,
who had been captured by the Hidatsa.
He offered to accompany us on our journey as an interpreter.
We would need horses to cross the mountains.
The Shoshone had great numbers of well-trained horses.
One of his wives could speak Shoshone.
She could translate when it came time to trade for horses.
Of course, he would be paid for their services.

Jessaume had already apprised us of Charbonneau's character.
He was a boastful and arrogant man,
living in the Mandan village,
where he was protected from the hostile tribes,
but he promised allegiance to no one but himself.
He was concerned mainly with profit from his trade—
trapping, hunting, and selling furs and hides.

We told Charbonneau we would think on his proposition.
He returned with his wife a few days later.
We were shocked to see her.
He had said she was a young woman,
but she was truly just a girl,
very young, perhaps fifteen or sixteen.
We could plainly see she was pregnant,
and from the rising mound below her belt,
we judged this baby would soon be born.
A young girl on a hazardous expedition with thirty young men
was cause enough for concern,
but now an infant, too . . .
Captain Lewis and I exchanged troubled glances.

Still, in consideration of the difficulties
we had incurred recently with the Sioux—
when lack of clear interpretation hindered our talks—
well, we were anxious to not repeat our blunders
and felt we had no other course of action open to us.

We definitely needed horses.
To have someone who could actually speak Shoshone
and who knew the people and possibly had relatives in the tribe,
we considered that a stroke of luck.
We would have to trust that it would somehow work out.

Plus, I have to admit that I was immediately
impressed by this squaw's manners.
She looked at us in a kindly, confident manner,
and she appeared quite eager to make this journey.
Perhaps the thought of seeing her own people was her true motivation.
Regardless, I had an instinctive feeling about her,
and both Lewis and I were delighted when she offered a gift,
a buffalo robe, she had sewn herself.
The next morning we sent word to Charbonneau
that his proposal was accepted, and we asked
that he move into our fort with his wife as soon as possible.

We moved from our camp into our lodging in late November,
despite the fact that we weren't completely finished.
It was not a minute too soon, for already it was brutally cold.
By early December, the Missouri River was completely frozen.
Our thermometers registered forty-five degrees below zero.

On December 25, Christmas, we celebrated
both the completion of the fort and the holiday itself.
Our men fired one round with the swivel gun.
A ration of rum was followed by a dinner
of the best meats that could be had.

On New Year's Day, we shared our merriment with the tribesmen.
The Indians performed a series of dances,
while their musicians played their tambourines and drums.
Pierre Cruzatte accompanied with his fiddle.
The Indians were much amused, especially when
Cruzatte laid his fiddle down and danced on his hands.

They were likewise enamored of York, who also danced.
They could hardly believe such a large and powerfully built man
could be so agile and lithe.

The Mandans informed us that they lacked for buffalo meat
to get through this early, brutal winter.
They held a buffalo dance for three straight evenings,
dancing in their finest clothes,
their rattles and drums providing sound and rhythm.
To our astonishment, they were rewarded just two days later
when a large herd of buffalo did appear.
I watched as the hunters, mounted on horseback
and armed with bows and arrows,
circled the herd, gradually driving them into the open fields.
Then the hunters rode in among them, singling out a female usually,
whom they wounded several times before the final, fatal stroke.
I was anxious to participate, and after observing for some time,
I joined the hunters and succeeded in killing ten of these animals myself.

In our travels to the villages, Lewis and I frequently
administered medical aid.
One small child had an abscess on his back.
Lewis was successful in his treatment.
The child's mother rewarded us
with as much corn as she could carry.
A young father brought his frostbit son.
Lewis administered the standard treatment to no avail.
He resorted to sawing off the boy's toes.
When the wounds had healed,
the father was happy to have him well
and took him back home in a sleigh.

Our most successful treatment came about
when Sacagawea, Charbonneau's young squaw,
went into labor on February 11.
This was her first child, and her labor was tedious and painful.

She cried out and suffered greatly throughout the night.
Charbonneau asked if there wasn't something
in our medicine box for his wife and child.
We frankly had nothing, but Jessaume came to our counsel
and advised that he had found that a small portion
of the rattle of a snake never failed to hasten a delivery.
Luckily, Lewis had two rattlesnake rings
in his cache of collected goods.
He broke them into small pieces and mixed them with water.
We helped Sacagawea to drink the mixture.
Within ten minutes, the child came forth—a fine, healthy boy.
There was never a more welcome sound
than the wails of life emitted by that child.
Cheers and applause erupted from the campfire gathering that evening.
Captain Lewis and I clapped each other on the back
and congratulated Charbonneau, the proud father.

We gathered much useful information while in the Mandan village.
The Hidatsa, who had traveled far in their raids,
were especially knowledgeable with regard to what lay to the west.
I made maps and endeavored to plot the best course.
Lewis took notes of the rivers we expected to encounter:
the White Earth River, the Yellowstone,
the Musselshell, and the Milk River,
which the Indians called "The River Which Scolds all Others."
We held some dread for the monstrous falls,
which the chiefs said we were destined to encounter.

In March we sat down with Charbonneau
to draw up the final contract for his employment.
We informed the Frenchman he would be required
to contribute to the physical labor of maintaining our camp
as well as to stand regular guard as the other men did.
Charbonneau was quite offended, declaring he would do no such things.
Furthermore, he had a list of his own demands.
He maintained that he would be free to leave the expedition at any time.

In addition, he retained the rights to ownership
of the furs and hides he trapped and hunted.
The profits made would be for him alone.

We flatly refused his demands.
Besides, we pointed out that we were highly suspicious
of his recent activities at the French trading posts,
for he had recently returned laden with gifts.
Perhaps these gifts were a bribe to enlist his aid against our purposes.
We ordered that he and his family
be immediately removed from our garrison.
He left in a huff and stayed away for several days,
but then a letter arrived by envoy.
It was an apology with a plea that we reconsider.
We sent for him and worked out a contract.
I was relieved, for I knew we needed the services of his squaw,
and I was aware of my growing attachment
to both Sacagawea and her son Jean Baptiste.

On March 22 it rained—our first rain of the season.
Ice on the river began to break up.
By the end of the month,
the river was a mass of floating ice and drowned buffalo.
The Indians jumped from one cake of ice to the next,
hauling in and harvesting as many corpses as they were able.

We constructed six more pirogues for our travel.
Then we packed the keelboat with cargo to present to Jefferson
and sent it back east with thirteen of our escorting party.
Included in this shipment were our ledgers and journals,
robust with the information we had accumulated.
Also, we sent botanical and mineral specimens,
all labeled as to when and where they were collected.
We included evidences of the animal life:
a stuffed male and female antelope
and skeletons of a weasel, a pronghorn, three Rocky Mountain squirrels,

various mice, and a marten.
We packed the horns of a mule deer and the skin of a weasel.
In addition, we sent live animals:
four magpies, a prairie dog, and a prairie grouse hen.

The keelboat set out on her return voyage to St. Louis on April 7.
We wasted no time with further goodbyes,
and Captain Lewis and I, with the remainder of the party,
set out in the opposite direction—up the waterway,
toward the branching rivers, the falls, and the mountains.

PART 3—ON THE TRAIL

April–May 1805
NORTH DAKOTA TO MONTANA

SACAGAWEA

I will tell you how it was traveling on our journey,
for I was the only woman in this tribe,
and I knew that I must come to know these men
so that I could judge their strengths and weaknesses
and become their friend.

The party was led by two chiefs.
Captain Lewis, whom the native peoples called Long Knife,
had golden hair like the sun.
Captain Clark was called Red Chief
because his hair was red like fire.
Both captains had for some time enjoyed the rank of manhood,
but still I thought them young.
My husband, Toussaint Charbonneau, a French Canadian trader,
had hair that was both black and white,
like the ashes of a fire pit.
He was the oldest man in this tribe.

Francois Labiche, George Drouillard, and Pierre Cruzatte
were men of mixed blood who spoke French, English,
and several of the native tongues.
All were good boatmen, hunters, and trappers.
Labiche was good at tracking horses, animals, and even people.
Cruzatte was always the favorite when we visited native villages,
for the tribesmen loved the music he made with his fiddle.
He had only one eye and turned his head
to one side when he looked at you.
George Gibson could play the fiddle likewise
and was the best man with a horse.
Patrick Gass was the chief when it was time to build the wooden huts.
Silas Goodrich could always catch the fish.

York was Captain Clark's slave.
His skin was black, and his hair curled tightly.
At first my people thought he had colored himself with coal,
but when they rubbed his skin and the color did not come off,
they realized black was his true skin color.
They were sure he shared the spirit of the buffalo and had great powers.
York and I worked side by side each day,
as we put up the teepee in the evening
and took it down in the morning.

Seaman was Captain Lewis's dog.
He was nearly the size of a black bear,
with just as much fur.
He loved to run along the path
and dive into bushes after rabbits and other game.
His favorite sport was to retrieve ducks and geese
when the captains shot them in the lake.
Captain Lewis loved his dog like one loves a brother or sister.

Charbonneau could hunt and fish and trap and interpret,
but he was not as valiant or skilled as the captains wished.
He was praised for his cooking, however,

especially when he cooked boudin blanc,
made by filling buffalo intestines with meat, fat, flour, and salt.
The sausage is then fried in fat till it is brown.
Boudin blanc was the favorite dish of the captains.

Of course, our youngest member was my son Jean Baptiste.
In the days when he was small,
I swaddled him in a blanket,
putting cat tail fluff and dried buffalo dung
in the bottom of his cradleboard.
This soaked up any wetness
and kept him warm and dry.
I laced him to the cradleboard
and then laced the cradleboard to my back.

Sometimes Charbonneau and I rode in the pirogue,
and sometimes we walked along the shore.
In the early days, our progress was slow,
for the water flowed one way
while we struggled to travel in the opposite direction.
The river was full of trees, stumps, rocks, and rapids.
Captain Clark often walked beside us
as he watched for large rocks.
Sometimes he would fall behind
and make funny faces at Jean Baptiste,
who would coo and babble in response.

I carried my digging stick,
and my eyes scouted about for edible plants.
I dug artichokes from underground holes
where the mice had hid them
and presented them to Captain Clark, who was delighted.
He also loved the sweet plant,
which he says tastes like licorice,
and the root plant, which is like a white apple.
I learned these English words from him and many others, too,

for he liked to be my teacher.
In return, I taught him native words and sign language.
We spent many hours conversing in our mixed-up language.

In the first days of travel,
Captain Clark referred to me as the "squaw woman,"
but when we became friends, he wished
to call me by name.
Sa-ca-ga-we-a, I repeated for him,
but his tongue stumbled over the sounds.
Nor did he like to call me by the English version of my name,
for he thought Bird Woman could only fit an old woman.
"I will call you Janey," he informed me,
and he wrote the word in his book and showed it to me.
I thought it a fine American name and did not protest.
He liked my name for Baptiste—Pomp,
and he often called him "my little Pompy."

Sometimes Charbonneau would stomp about
as if he were angry that Captain Clark and I shared good times,
and then Captain Clark would turn and ask him for stories
of his travels and his hunting and trapping.
Although Charbonneau could not speak English well,
still the words flowed from his mouth,
and it would be a long while before his mouth was closed again,
for he loved to talk of his adventures.

The captains and the men had many tasks.
Their days were busy with walking, rowing, hunting,
fishing, cooking, repairing clothes and canoes.
But the most important task
the Great White Father had charged them with
was to make a record of their journey.
They did so by making marks in their books
and by drawing maps and making sketches.
Captain Clark showed me many pictures

of prairie dogs and elk and horned sheep
and antelope and buffalo.
The Great White Father had never seen such creatures,
I was told, for they did not live on the other side of the Mississippi.

The men enjoyed hunting in the first days of the journey,
and we were never without meat.
They were eager to bring down a grizzly bear.
I tried to warn them about the dangers of this animal,
for they did not understand his strength or ferocity.
The bear is a proud animal
who will quickly take revenge upon a hunter.
My own Shoshone cousin was killed when a grizzly bear
chased and overtook him at the edge of the prairie.
There were seven warriors in the hunting party,
but none of them could distract or kill the bear.
So I was not surprised when Charbonneau returned
with the story of how the bear chased him down the creek.
He was saved only by the shot from Cruzatte's gun.
After several such occasions,
the men were not so eager to find the grizzly.

The animal that delighted us all
was the pronghorn antelope,
who is not at all fierce
but is as difficult to kill as the grizzly,
for he is a shy and watchful creature
who stays in the high places.
He has a keen sight and a keen sense of smell.
Our hunters would carefully and quietly approach a herd,
only to have the antelope flee easily to a farther location.
Their flight across the land was so quick
that we could hardly see their legs.
They resembled huge birds, flying across the land.
I thought them the most beautiful and graceful creatures.

We enjoyed many fair days with gentle breezes.
On one such day, we admired
orange and yellow flowers blooming on the bank
and the dome of blue sky with scattered clouds of white.
The sun shone warm upon our skin.
Charbonneau and I rode in the pirogue on this day,
our sail hoisted to catch the wind.
The captains walked along the shore, discussing future days,
when suddenly we noticed darkness at the edge of the sky.
The darkness approached and grew until it filled the sky.
Angry clouds were piled on top of one another,
and bolts of lightning shot out from the darkness.
A mighty wind seized our sail,
and strong rains pounded us from above.
Our boat keeled to one side.
Charbonneau, who was at the helm, was then a crazy man.
He steered the boat into the wind
when he should have turned the boat around it.
The boat turned on its side, and water poured in.
Charbonneau stood and shouted prayers,
beseeching his god to come down and save him,
for he could not swim if this boat was turned over.
The boat rocked from side to side as he stood,
the sail making loud, flapping noises.

As the water came into the boat,
the items that were in it floated out.
These were things prized by our captains:
food, maps, important papers, instruments, medicine,
and presents intended for the native peoples.
All were floating out as Charbonneau stood and yelled.
Captain Lewis fired his gun into the air
and commanded Charbonneau to take the tiller,
but still he didn't.
Captain Clark ordered Cruzatte to take over.
Cruzatte ordered Charbonneau to sit down or be shot.

Charbonneau was as much afraid of being shot
as of falling into the water,
so he sat down and took the tiller.
The sail was brought in and order was restored.
Two of the men scooped the water out with cooking vessels,
and finally we paddled ashore.
While all of the madness was happening around me,
I had leaned over and retrieved many things—
papers, instruments, and medicine.
Captain Lewis was especially grateful that I had saved his papers.
He had spent many hours working on them,
for they were to be delivered
to the Great White Chief in Washington.
We spread all of the wet things on a dry blanket
in a high place sheltered by large rocks.
The warming rays of the sun did their work,
and soon enough the items were dried and returned to the boat.

Captain Lewis was much relieved, and he declared a time of celebration.
Bottles of whiskey were opened and passed around.
Over the next few days, we traveled to the Musselshell River,
where the winds were calm.
We came upon a beautiful stream.
Captain Lewis declared that this stream would be called Sacagawea River,
to honor the good work I had done for our group.
I myself saw the marks of my name with the other words
in the book the Captain kept.

In the fair days that followed,
we came to a land of enchantment;
I judged it to be a sacred land.
The cliffs along the shore were made of beautiful, white stone
with jagged edges touching the blue sky.
Flocks of birds lived in these cliffs.
They swooped out from overhangs and cried out to us.
I removed Baptiste from his cradleboard and pointed to the sky.

His eyes followed the birds as they careened through the air.
He returned their call with his own high-pitched cry.

April–May 1805
NORTH DAKOTA TO MONTANA

CLARK

My fears about the burden of Charbonneau's squaw and infant
were immediately abated on the first evening of our journey,
for no sooner had we halted for dinner than I noted
she was walking about with her digging stick,
searching for wild artichokes,
which had been hidden and hoarded away by the field mice.
Her findings were a welcome addition to our meat-filled diet.
As we proceeded, she pointed out berries,
found in abundance in the bottomlands.
She also found a sweet plant that we called wild licorice.
She herself was fond of a root
that we called the white apple, a starchy tuber.
The apple itself was a bit too coarse for our diet,
but the root served as a thickener when added to soups and gravies.

We found Charbonneau to be of some merit with his cooking skills.
He had the knack of the French cook
with his various seasonings and sauces.
Captain Lewis and I both richly enjoyed his prized boudin blanc,

a type of sausage made from a fat buffalo.
We were quite taken by the artistry by which he
accomplished this tasty treat.
Beginning with six feet or so of the buffalo intestine,
Charbonneau carefully squeezed until it was emptied.
He then kneaded filets and portions of shoulder meat
with a portion of kidney suet.
Pepper, salt, and flour were added.
The intestine casing, which has never touched water
(for that would ruin the taste),
is then tied at one end and turned inward
with a rotating motion of his hand and arm
and a brisk motion of the thumb and forefinger.
He puts in what he says is "bon pour manger," or *good to eat.*
He continues stuffing and compressing
until the casing is nearly bursting to its limit.
Then it is tied at the other end and baptized in the Missouri
with two dips and a "flirt,"
after which it is bobbed into the kettle and boiled.
Finally, it is browned in bear's oil.
This sumptuous fare was held in high esteem by all of us.

I acquired the habit of spending a good part of the day
walking on the land in the company of Charbonneau and Sacagawea
and the baby, whom Charbonneau called Baptiste.
I quite preferred Sacagawea's name for him—Pomp,
which I understood meant "firstborn."
The infant had grown into an alert and curious baby
during this part of our journey.
His eyes, large and dark, paused to take in
whatever or whomever was before him.
He made cooing noises when I talked to him
and entertained us all by blowing bubbles with his spittle.

Sacagawea—I found her both inquisitive and bright.
She was a ready pupil as well as a teacher.

She delighted in showing off her knowledge of edible plant life,
and she insisted I teach her English words
for objects she pointed out to me.
We communicated by sign language quite well.
I noticed she had mastered a working vocabulary of French,
as she seemed to understand Charbonneau when he spoke with Drouillard.

As our journey continued, we found ourselves entranced
by beautiful stretches of land, barren of tree or bush
for as far as the eye could see.
The soil we deemed rich, however,
as evidenced by the abundant grasses.
Indeed, this was a paradise to all life.
We sighted many deer, elk, buffalo, sheep, pronghorn,
beaver, fox, wolf, and bear.
We hunted, killed, and dressed meat and ate well,
taking only what was needed and being grateful for the abundance.

Our men were most anxious to take a grizzly.
All of the Indians we had met had warned us
about the difficult nature of the task.
Their ventures were all preceded by much ceremony and painting.
They never attempted a kill with less than a party of six or eight men.
Even with all of their precautions,
they informed us that it was often common to lose a man.
But our men were not so easily discouraged.
They pointed out that the Indian was forced into close proximity
because he was limited to weapons of bows and arrows
and poor shooting rifles.
We would not be in such jeopardy with our powerful guns.

They were mistaken.
Private Bratton fired and wounded a grizzly,
which then turned on him and pursued him for quite a distance.
Bratton flagged the pirogue down,
and Lewis ordered the crew to pursue the monster.

They tracked him for a mile through thick brush
and finally brought him down with two shots to the head.
Upon further examination, we noted
that Bratton's shot had penetrated his lungs.
We were all astounded that this bear
could have run such a distance in his wounded state.

Three days later, Drouillard, Charbonneau, and four other men
snuck up to within forty yards of a grizzly.
Four of the men fired simultaneously.
All four balls hit the mark,
two of them piercing the bear's lung.
Nevertheless, the bear rose with a roar and charged,
his mouth open and his teeth bared.
The two men who had been held in reserve fired,
hitting the bear's shoulder.
The men were on the run then.
Two managed to escape in canoes.
Drouillard and Charbonneau hid in the willows.
The bear proceeded to rout them out.
Both men threw down their rifles and pouches
and dove into the river from a bank.
The bear charged after them.
He was about to reach Charbonneau
when Drouillard retrieved his gun and
shot through the bear's head, killing him.

Several weeks passed when I found myself
in the midst of a fray with a grizzly.
Drouillard and I were on patrol that day.
We put five balls into his head and five in various other parts
before we brought him down.
From the very first shot to his dying breath,
he made the most dreadful roar.
I judged him to weigh at least five hundred pounds.
Lewis argued that it was six.

We found the men's curiosity considerably diminished after that,
and our pattern of behavior toward the grizzly
turned from one of seeking to one of avoidance.

I would have counted the bear encounters
as our greatest horror during this period
had it not been for the near disaster we suffered
with our most prized sailing vessel.
We captains traveled by means of the white pirogue.
It was slightly smaller than the red and more stable.
It carried our astronomical instruments, our medicines,
our best trade goods, our writing desks, our journals,
and several casks of gun powder.
The usual procedure was for either Lewis or me
to always to be on deck,
while the other walked ahead on the bank,
watching for impediments in the river.
But that day, being such a pleasant day,
Lewis and I thought better to spend time
discussing future plans as we walked together.

A sudden squall of wind descended upon us with no warning.
Charbonneau, our poorest navigator by far, was at the helm.
He immediately panicked, and instead of putting the ship
before the wind, he lofted her up into it.
The wind was so strong that it forced the brace of the sail
out of the hand of the attending man.
Our vessel, upset and on her side,
began to fill with water before she could be righted.
We watched in horror as our treasured items floated out.
Charbonneau was of further detriment in his anguished state.
He stood up and cried to God for mercy,
fearing for his own life because he could not swim.

Cruzatte maintained his wits and threatened to shoot Charbonneau
if he could not sit down and regain his composure.

I believed he would have, too.
Fortunately, Charbonneau resumed his seat,
took the tiller, and the pirogue righted.
Still, the vessel was half-filled with water.
Cruzatte and others immediately began bailing with kettles.
In the midst of all the chaos and confusion,
Sacagawea sat, calm and serene.
Quietly, she leaned over and retrieved
nearly everything that had gone overboard.
Thankfully, she thought to do this,
for no one else amidst all the upheaval had the wits to do so.
The result was we lost very few articles—
a bit of medicine, gunpowder, and some garden seeds.
After two days of sun, most of the supplies had dried
and were restored and repacked into the boat.

Such was our gratitude to Sacagawea that a few days later,
we named a portion of the Musselshell River after her.
I wrote it in the ledger for her to see—Birdwoman's River,
Birdwoman being the English equivalent of her name, Sacagawea.

Lewis told me later that the incident remained fresh in his mind
for weeks with all of the original horror and dread.
I was inclined to agree that it was indeed a fearful time,
but the picture that has stayed in my mind is the one
of Sacagawea—composed and collected—
accomplishing the tasks that needed to be done.
I judged her at that time to be as brave, clear-headed,
and reliable as any our finest soldiers
and counted myself lucky that we had her in our company.

The land formations encountered during this section of our journey
were quite rugged and beautiful,
like nothing we had ever seen before
or that we would have even dreamed existed in this continent.
Pitched, high-rising bluffs in shades of brown

formed a stark contrast to the blue sky and the blazing sun.
I called these lands the Deserts of America.
I doubted that they would ever be habitable.
The air was the driest we had ever encountered,
our ink wells drying before we could finish writing.

Here we made the acquaintance of an animal
the French call the rock mountain sheep.
It is about the size of a large deer or small elk.
The horns are thick and large and wind around the head.

In late May, Lewis and I scaled the eastern end of the breaks.
We saw for the first time the distant Rocky Mountains,
the tops of which were covered with snow.
We found our spirits lifted by the sight,
knowing that we were nearing the headwaters of the Missouri,
and yet our joy was leveled by our knowledge
of the hardships that lay before us.

Progress on the river during this period
was slow because of the high bluffs,
the numerous bends in the river, the winds,
the protruding rocks, and the shallow waters.
We were obliged to travel mostly by means
of pulling the pirogues and canoes with elk-skin ropes.
We endured a traumatic incident when on the last day of May,
the tow rope of the white pirogue broke.
The pirogue swung out and nearly crashed into a rock.
We judged ourselves lucky that it was not smashed and splintered.
A cause for celebration, we gave each man a dram of refreshment.

May–July 1805
NORTHERN MONTANA

SACAGAWEA

We camped in a place where the air was dry.
The wooden case, where the medicine was kept,
shrank and was hard to open.
Captain Clark showed me that his ink dried so quickly
that he could scarcely make marks on his paper.

When we came to a fork in the river,
the captains weren't sure which turn to follow.
Did the main river flow north or south?
Captain Lewis determined that we should travel on the south water
because it was wider with a stronger current.
The men did not agree, but they respected the captains' decisions,
and we set about on the southern river.

When we spotted smoke rising in the distance,
the captains puzzled over what caused it.
It did not look like the smoke of campfires.
Perhaps this smoke was made by the vapor of water,
and perhaps it would lead us to the place of the Great Falls.

The native people had informed the captains
that when they found these falls,
they would know they were on the right road
to the mountains and the river that flowed to the Big Waters.
Captain Lewis struck out with a group of men
to investigate the rising smoke.

Captain Clark remained behind
with Charbonneau and me and the rest of the men.
While we were setting up camp that evening,
lightning hit the tree behind our tent.
The tree suddenly blazed with fire.
It fell, nearly crashing into our tent.
York and I quickly moved the tent so that it was saved,
and then we sat and stared at the burning log
and considered what our fate would have been
if we had not acted so quickly.

Later that same evening, I fell ill.
At first, it was only a simple ache in my side.
I rubbed the place that hurt and took deep breaths.
But when I retired, it became a burning pain,
so fierce that I could think of nothing else.
I held my breath and struggled to keep
from crying out and awaking the others.
When Baptiste nursed, I trembled and moaned.
Charbonneau came and sat behind me,
propping me up in his arms to steady my shaking.
Baptiste drank his fill and drifted off again to sleep.
But the next day the terrible pain was still present.
I could not carry Baptiste or anything else on my back.
I could not dig for roots;
I could not build fires;
I could only lie on my elk hide
while the pain persisted and a fever raged.
I tried to nurse Jean Baptiste,

but I could not eat myself.
Soon, I knew, I would have no milk for Pompy, my firstborn.

Captain Clark came to check on me throughout the day.
Although his words were encouraging,
his blue eyes were dull pools, and he did not smile.
That evening he made the cut of a knife on my arm
to allow the blood to leak poison from my body.
Then he made a poultice of bark,
which he laid below my stomach.
But I think there was still much poison in my body,
for I continued to be in great pain.
Next he gave me medicine of quinine from his medicine box.
I would not take it because of the bitter taste
until he mixed it with water sweetened with a sugar cube.
My pain eased some then, but still I was very sick.

When Captain Lewis returned from his explorations on the river,
he gave me a new medicine—laudanum.
For six more days I remained sick on my elk hide,
my eyes closed to the life around me.
My mind traveled, however, to the spirit world,
where I walked around a gray lake,
which was shrouded by white shadows.
Other spirits walked alongside me, although we did not speak.

When I awoke, I was thirsty.
Captain Lewis ordered that I drink water from a nearby spring.
There is big medicine, he insisted, in the spring water.
Surely it would make me well.
The day after I drank the spring water,
my pain eased and the burning in my head ceased.
I was very hungry then.
Captain Lewis instructed others to feed me
small bits of buffalo meat and broth,
and every day I should continue to drink water from the stream.

I ate as Captain Lewis directed, but still I was hungry.
When the captains were busy with their other duties,
I asked Charbonneau to bring me white apple roots and dried fish.
I ate freely of them, and then I was sick again.
The captains were very angry
but not with me—with Charbonneau,
for I had been left in his charge.
I protested to the captains and pointed to myself
to show them it was my fault.
But still they stabbed their fingers toward Charbonneau
and made angry faces at him.

We learned from Captain Lewis that he had followed
the rising smoke until they came to the place of the Great Falls.
As soon as I was well enough,
we hastened to travel to it.
As we approached, we heard a gentle roar
that became louder and louder
until we could hear no other noises.
When we arrived, we saw how it was so,
for there before us was a monstrous falls,
where water crashed down and spilled over huge rocks.
As soon as the water hit these rocks,
it danced back up, rising on long legs high into the air.
As we moved in closer, we were bathed in the spray,
so we moved back to a farther point,
where we observed clouds floating over the falls.
Suddenly, a rainbow of red, yellow, blue, and green appeared
and spread across the mist.
We were small people compared to this great falls.
We stood in wonder and did not speak for some time.

But soon enough, heavier thoughts weighed upon us,
for we realized that we could not cross the falls on foot.
We would have to put all of our possessions
on our backs and also carry our boats.

The men built wooden wagons to help them
drag the canoes across the land.
The heavier boats we had to leave behind.

One of our worst days came
when we were walking peacefully along the riverbank.
Suddenly, the wind began to make a whistling noise.
Captain Clark pointed to the thunderclouds,
appearing like mountains in the distance.
Jagged flashes of lightning crackled in the sky.
Captain Clark directed us to take refuge in a gully.
We would stay there until the storm passed.
At first, the rain descended upon us in large spatters,
but then it came in heavy gushes with balls of pounding ice.

We huddled closely together, hoping it would soon be over.
But the gully was no longer a safe place,
for torrents of muddy water and giant boulders pursued us.
Soon the water was around our waists,
pushing and pulling us with such a force
that our clothes, belts, knives, and backpacks were torn away.
I quickly undid Pomp from the cradleboard
and locked my arms around him.
His cradle, the mosquito netting, and all of his clothes
were wrenched from my grasp and swept away,
but I held on fiercely to Jean Baptiste.

Charbonneau was crazy with fear.
He tried to scramble up the side.
As he did, he dropped his gun, his shot pouch, his horn, his tomahawk,
and even Captain Clark's compass—
all were swept into the raging waters.
Captain Clark rescued Charbonneau by standing behind him
and shoving him up out of the gully.
And then Captain Clark also gathered Pomp and me
and pushed us up so that we, too, were standing on top.

We all looked down then at the wild, rolling, brown water,
and we knew that if we had been in it for a few moments more,
we would have been swept away.
And like the water, rocks, tree stumps, and our possessions,
we also would have plunged over the mighty falls.

I was very cold then, and my body began to shiver.
Captain Clark gave me a drink of rum,
which normally only the soldiers drink,
but he said I must drink it to stay warm,
for he feared that if I didn't, I would be sick again.
I felt the rush of warmth as the rum rushed through my blood,
and I hugged my naked Baptiste to my chest.

We traveled for thirty days around these falls,
carrying all of our possessions, including the boats.
We often walked on ground that was covered with prickly cactus,
which tore at our moccasins and wounded our feet.
In the evening, I helped the men to mend their moccasins
while the captains applied medicines to their feet.

When finally the falls were behind us,
Captain Lewis climbed to the top of a high hill
and looked westward with his looking glass.
Surely, he would now be able to see the waterway that traveled west,
that would take us to the Big Waters.
But he returned with a sad face.
No, he had not seen such a passageway.
The men were all saddened.
Surely we were lost, they thought,
or perhaps such a passageway did not exist.
Then how could we make our way to the Big Waters?

May–July 1805
NORTHERN MONTANA

CLARK

On the morning of June 3,
we found ourselves faced with a critical decision,
as we were now positioned at the junction of two large rivers,
only one of which could be the Missouri.
The men all believed the north fork to be the Missouri,
as it ran in the same boiling and rolling manner,
and its waters were the same whitish-brown color.
The south, by contrast, was perfectly transparent
and ran smooth and unruffled.
Lewis and I, nevertheless, felt unsure
and split up to explore the two alternatives.
We decided that the southern branch,
which was wider and had stronger currents,
must be the correct choice.
The men were all—to the last one—sure that we were making a mistake.
Nevertheless, they cheerfully and faithfully honored our decision.

The Indians had all told us we should come to a great falls
before we reached the mountains,

but after nearly a week of travel, we still had not reached it.
Lewis decided it best if he set out in search with a small party.
A letter from him arrived on June 13,
informing us that our choice of route was the correct one
and that he and his men had arrived at the falls.

Of course, this was good news,
but I feared a graver matter was now upon us,
for Sacagawea had taken ill.
Her condition deteriorated miserably over a period of several days.
She lay on her elk hide, moaning and turning this way and that.
Jean Baptiste's cries could be heard throughout the camp,
for his mother could not nurse him properly.
Charbonneau and I took turns walking about with him.
We dipped a cloth in sugar water and urged him to suck
between his meager feedings.

I made small cuts with a knife and bled Sacagawea,
as was the standard practice.
In addition, I applied a poultice of Peruvian bark
and laudanum to her abdomen.
I saw no relief, so I was heartily glad when Lewis arrived and took over.
He noted her high fever, her very weak pulse,
her irregular breathing, and the twitching of her fingers and arms.

Lewis prescribed two doses of bark and opium,
which worked marvelously for her pulse.
She complained of great thirst, however.
Lewis remembered a sulphur spring he had passed
and insisted that the men fetch water from it.
He recalled such a spring back east, which contained iron and sulphur,
and was widely regarded for its healing tonic.
She drank eagerly and soon showed remarkable signs of improvement,
much to our relief.
Lewis prescribed a diet of salted, peppered, broiled buffalo meat,

giving strict instructions to Charbonneau
that she was to have nothing else.

The next morning, however,
she was extremely hungry after her meal
and she persuaded Charbonneau to provide her
with white apples and some dried fish.
She became quite ill again.
Lewis and I were both furious with Charbonneau,
and Lewis strongly reprimanded him.
I held my tongue for fear of what might erupt with my anger.
Lewis then gave Sacagawea broken doses of diluted niter,
followed by thirty drops of laudanum.
She had a restful evening.
At morning, her fever appeared to have diminished.
She declared herself free from pain,
and indeed, she was up and about, walking and fishing.
I was much relieved.

Only then did we give our attention to our next task,
which was to scout out the falls
and determine the best route for portage.
Proceeding upriver, we passed a succession of rapids and cascades.
We heard the roar for several miles
before we actually reached the site.
Once there, we were quite astounded by the cataracts.
Water pitched over a cliff and fell for more than ninety feet
to rocks below, creating a splendid dance of foam.
From the foot of the falls arose a continuous mist.
As the sun penetrated the clouds,
we were delighted to see a rainbow.
Upon further exploration, we soon enough discovered
that what we had thought was one great fall
was actually five waterfalls.

We knew we could not carry the canoes and supplies
across our backs on this rough land,
so we built two wagons.
I was lucky enough to find a large cottonwood
that amply provided material for our wheels.
We proceeded across rough terrain with a series
of maneuvers that included pushing, hoisting, letting down, and pulling.
We even raised the mast and sails on the canoes
in an attempt to harness the wind to come to our aid.

The greatest nuisance during this segment was the prickly pear cactus,
which grew abundantly on the ground.
These barbed menaces tore unmercifully at our moccasins and feet.
The men, by necessity, sewed new moccasins every two days,
putting on double soles and even mending them every other night.

Other hardships added to our trials.
We had several breakdowns of equipment, which halted our progress.
One day we were assaulted by hail the size of apples.
Mosquitoes were a constant nuisance in the evenings.
Days of burning hot sun were distressing,
as were other days of freezing, cold rains.
Large herds of buffalo impeded our progress.
Grizzlies were numerous and threatening.

On June 29, we experienced a storm so severe
that our lives were in peril.
We were walking pleasantly enough along the riverbank
when the wind produced a loud-pitched, whistling noise.
I noted thunderclouds building on the horizon.
Knowing that a storm would soon be upon us,
I directed our group to take refuge in a gully,
where we could huddle and stay dry beneath overhanging rocks.

We had no sooner settled ourselves
when a loud clap of thunder assaulted our ears.

A slow, easy rain increased in intensity and volume.
Large stones of hail soon rained down upon us.
Suddenly the gully began to fill with water.
A loud, rumbling noise brought further terror.
I peered out from under the rocks
to see an enormous wave of muddy water roaring down the ravine.
Large slabs of mud and giant boulders rushed toward us.
In a matter of seconds, the water was at our waists.
Charbonneau was frozen with fear,
but I managed to shove him up the side of the gully.
I then grabbed my gun in one hand
and braced myself behind Sacagawea and the baby Baptiste.
I steadily pushed them toward the top.

When we were all safely at the summit,
we risked looking down at the raging waters.
I knew that a quarter of a mile ahead
the main river dropped into another steep waterfall.
If we had not escaped the gully,
the charging waters would have carried us to that fate.
Sacagawea lost Baptiste's cradleboard
and all of his clothes and bedding.
Although the baby was alarmed, he appeared to be well.
I lost a most valued item—my compass.
Fortunately, I recovered it several days later.
Sacagawea, meanwhile, had begun to shiver with damp and cold.
I wasted no time in administering a sip of whiskey to her.
I worried that her fever and illness might return,
and for the next few days, I kept a close vigil on her.

We took our nation's birth date, July 4, as a working day,
but in the evening, we gave each of the men a gill of whiskey.
It was the last of our stock.
Cruzatte played the fiddle, and the men danced quite merrily.
Our dinner that evening was a comfortable enough one
of bacon, beans, suit dumpling, and buffalo beef.

We resumed our trek the following day, July 5.
We had originally allotted a period of a week for our portage,
but in actuality, we spent a full month traveling around these falls.
On July 12, we set out for the mountains.

Beginning on July 23, Captain Lewis attempted
to bring to fruition his dream of the *iron boat*.
He had designed a collapsible canoe of iron in ten sections.
We had carried it with us thus far.
Our task at this point was to add wood ribs
and a covering of animal hides,
which would be stretched around for the boat's "skin."
When the task was completed, much to Lewis's joy,
the iron boat floated like a perfect cork on the water,
at least for a short time.
After that, unfortunately, it sank.
Lewis was quite shattered.
He attributed the failure to the error
of making the seam holes too big
as well as the lack of proper sealer.
We were unable to find pine trees to extract a pine pitch sealer.
Instead, he had used a mixture of beeswax, tallow, and charcoal dust.

I had actually anticipated such a failure
but had not the heart to dampen Lewis's enthusiasm.
I had, however, quietly sent my hunters out
in search for large trees to build canoes.
We succeeded in building two large ones,
which we added to our fleet of six smaller ones.
We set out with the hope that the river
would penetrate the land to the point of the Continental Divide,
where we would meet the Shoshone Indians
and secure the horses needed to make
the overland trip across the mountains.

PART 5—THE SHOSHONE

July–August 1805
ACROSS MONTANA INTO IDAHO

SACAGAWEA

Yes, the soldiers were worried
about not finding the waters that would carry us to the Big Lake.
My own spirit was not so troubled, however,
because as we traveled, I felt the kinship
of a land that I had once known.
The smell of the earth,
the red berries that covered the bushes,
the sunflowers that grew along the river—
yes, these sights and scents were familiar.
I showed our captains how the sunflower seeds
could be put to good use by grinding them with rock
and mixing some of the powder with water to make a drink.
The rest of the powder I dumped into a bowl with oil
and stirred until I had a dough to bake.

We came upon campfire ashes and found
a pair of moccasins and an old pot left behind.
These were not Shoshone, I announced.

69

The captains were disappointed,
but I was not disheartened, for still I felt this was the land of my people.

When I saw the beaver head rising from the flat land,
then my feelings were confirmed.
Yes, I knew that rock formation.
We had called it Beaverhead Rock because
the rock resembled the head of the beaver swimming in the stream.
This, I informed the captains, is the buffalo hunting land of my people.
When we come to the three forks in the river, I declared,
then we will be at the place where I was captured by the Hidatsa warriors.

Captain Lewis was anxious to find my people.
He announced that he would travel at a faster pace, ahead of our group.
I instructed him to announce himself as a man of peace,
by putting his gun down and offering his blanket in friendship.
All native peoples recognize this sign.
If these people appeared agreeable,
then Lewis should paint their cheeks with red paint,
for red is the color of peace,
while black is the color of war.

Captain Lewis took several men and hurried forward.
We followed behind at a slower pace.
My thoughts of happiness were interrupted
only by the rattlesnake who leapt from the bushes.
We had heard no warning rattle,
for we had not intruded into his territory.
I was filled with fear as I saw his fangs coming forward,
but Captain Clark quickly brought his foot in front of mine.
With a swift shot from his gun,
he killed the angry snake, whose head splattered at our feet.
My heart pounded, and Baptiste cried loudly
and would not be comforted for some time.

Charbonneau was angered because I had walked so close
to the bush with the rattlesnake.
Surely, there had been a warning rattle.
Perhaps I was distracted by this constant talking with Captain Clark.
I knew that was not the problem, so I said nothing.
But still, when Baptiste continued to cry,
Charbonneau struck me, the flat of his hand smacking my cheek.

Captain Clark was then a man of fury.
With three quick strides, he was in front of Charbonneau.
I thought he might raise his hand, but he restrained himself.
He delivered a scolding speech,
first shaking his finger in Charbonneau's face,
then throwing his hands into the air and kicking the ground.
Charbonneau said nothing in return but remained facing him,
his own angry eyes matching Captain Clark's.
Captain Clark spewed forth more words
until Charbonneau's head bowed.
Only then did Captain Clark resume his walk.
We followed behind him, not speaking with each other.
Baptiste had ceased his piercing cries by this time.
I wondered then about how it was in the villages
where the white people lived.
Perhaps in these towns, men are not allowed to strike their women.

The next morning, we resumed our travels.
The men rowed the boats along the river.
Charbonneau and I walked along the shore, Baptiste on my back.
Captain Clark walked behind us.
Soon enough, I saw figures in the distance.
And as they came closer,
I knew these were my people, for they were not tall,
and their hair was worn loosely, not bound or braided.
They wore moccasins and dresses of deer, elk, and buffalo skin.
When they were closer, I could see the shells, dangling from their ears.
Yes, these were my people!

I could not contain my joy!
I jumped into the air and raised my arms to the sky.
I danced in small circles.
I looked back to Captain Clark
and pointed to the people in the distance.
I put my fingers to my lips to show
that these were the people who first gave me nourishment.

As they drew nearer, it appeared
that the entire village had come to greet us.
When Captain Drouillard appeared over the rise,
we guessed that Captain Lewis had been in the Shoshone village
and had sent Drouillard with these people to find and greet us.

One of the younger women broke from the crowd
and came running toward me,
and then my joy was beyond belief,
for it was Jumping Fish!
Jumping Fish--who had been captured with me that day many years ago.
How could this be? Somehow she had escaped,
and she had made the long journey back.
It hardly seemed possible that she could be here,
that we would be reunited with each other.
We embraced and tears ran down our cheeks.
We danced and cried out our happiness.
Perhaps the white soldiers thought we were crazy,
but there were smiles upon their faces too.

We then walked all in one group to the village,
and I proudly showed off my baby Baptiste,
who jabbered and looked about with bright, shining eyes.
Memories of days past flooded my thoughts,
and I began to inquire about the people I had known.
Soon a circle of old friends gathered around me,
but I was allowed only a short time to visit
because then it was time for the talks,

and my services were needed to interpret.
York came to escort me to the head teepee.

When I entered the tepee, I kept my head down,
for women are not allowed to sit as equals in the council meetings.
Our captains were seated in a circle with the chiefs of the tribe.
Their moccasins had been removed,
and I quickly removed mine.
It is a gesture of good will to remove moccasins,
for if anyone should break a promise made before the council fire,
then he would surely go barefoot for the rest of his life.

My eyes darted to Captain Clark to await instruction.
He was seated on a white robe with six white shells tied in his hair.
The flap of the tent was opened again
as the head chief of the tribe entered.
He lowered himself to his seat and also removed his shoes.
When he began to speak, I lifted my eyes in surprise.
He had a low voice that reminded me of the sound
of gentle winds blowing through the tall reeds of the river.
His eyes were dark brown with circles of gold in the middle.
His nose had a bump below the brow, just like that of my father.

"Cameahwait!" I exclaimed, "my brother!"
My emotions could not be held back—
they broke forth like the raging waters
of the mountain stream that overflows its banks
during heavy spring rains.
I could not restrain myself.
I rushed forward and threw my blanket around him
to show that he and I were born of the same mother and father.
My own brother! I had not seen him since we were children.
I had feared that he had been killed during the raid.
He was alive and well and chief of the village!
He returned my embrace, and we spoke words of comfort.
I did not want to part with him,

but he gently removed my arms from his neck,
and I understood that I was to resume my place.
These talks must move forward.
But still, as I spoke, I could not control
the stream of tears that flowed down my cheeks.

Our captains explained that there was a new father in this land.
He resided in the head village far away, in the lands to the east.
They—Chief Lewis and Chief Clark—
had been sent to explore his new land.
It was the white chief's desire to open the road to the Big Waters.
It would be a road of peace for people of all colors.
The Great Father in the East would now be the father to them also.
He would make sure that they had provisions and lived in peace.

Of course, it was not a simple manner to pass these words on,
for the captains spoke in English.
The soldier Labiche said the words in French to Charbonneau.
Charbonneau told them to me in Hidatsa,
and I pronounced the Shoshone words
that carried these thoughts to our chiefs.
In this manner, the talks proceeded.

When the captains judged that enough talk
had been made for one day,
they presented the chiefs with round medals of gold.
To Cameahwait, they gave the medal
with the picture of Jefferson, the Great White Father, on one side.
On the other side of the coin appeared a pipe and tomahawk
and two hands clasped in friendship.
Captain Clark then unfolded the flag
with red and white stripes and stars in the blue night.

If the Shoshone would follow their counsel, Captain Clark promised,
then they would live long lives and outnumber the trees in the forest.
Other gifts would follow, he promised—whiskey, guns, tobacco.

But he and his men would need horses to cross the great mountains,
and they hoped that the Shoshone would provide them with fine steeds.

Many agreements and promises were made.
When the captains and chiefs departed,
I was given time alone with my brother.
I gave him a lump of sugar.
He thought it glistened like new fallen snow.
It was the most pleasing thing he had ever tasted, he declared.

We talked of my life with the Hidatsa
and of his life as chief of the village.
I spoke of my fine baby Baptiste,
and he told me of his own children.
What of our sister, our brother, our father, our mother?
I finally asked the questions that weighed upon me.
Where could I find them?
He bowed his head and sat for a moment in silence.
Then he spoke the words: "Most of our family is gone."
When he raised his eyes, I saw the sadness that remained.
"They did not survive the raid when you were taken.
In some ways, Sacagawea,
it was your good fortune to be a captive
because many of the village did not survive.
One child from our family remains from that day of horror."
Cameahwait called to one of his warriors to bring this child,
and I was presented with my sister's son, whom I hugged fiercely.
"You are now my son," I assured him. "I will be your mother."

I was then allowed more time to show off
both my new son and my baby Baptiste.
I walked through the village and greeted people,
some of them friends from my earlier life.
I noticed that an older brave followed me, staying several paces behind.
Each time I turned, I saw him standing behind me.

Finally, I faced him with a questioning eye.
He looked familiar, but I could not place him.

"I was to be your husband," he insisted
as he looked at me, his eyes going up and down.
I did not judge his look to be a friendly one.
Rather, he seemed angry.
And then I remembered that, yes, I had been promised,
and horses and mules had been paid to my family
for the promise of my skills as young wife and mother,
but this man could surely see the child upon my back now.
As we spoke, Charbonneau, tall and big like a grizzly bear, appeared,
his knife in his belt, his rifle at his side.

"So," White Rabbit began, for I then remembered his name,
"you have returned. I now have two wives and several children.
I will not provide for you. I no longer want you for a wife."
Before I could make an answer, he turned his back
and with quick, even steps strode to his teepee.

In the days that followed, the talks continued.
My brother Cameahwait was a great help to our captains.
He drew a wavy line in the sand to demonstrate the river.
Then he piled sand high to show the mountains
that would have to be crossed.
He had never crossed these mountains,
but there was one man in the tribe, Old Toby,
who could guide them if he should agree to go.
Cameahwait informed them that the Nez Perce Indians
inhabited the river land that ran at the foot of the mountains.
These people reported that their river ran
a great way toward the setting sun,
and then it emptied to a great lake
that reached as far as the eye could see.
The water of this lake tasted very ill and could not be drunk.
Our Captains were then excited because they believed this

to be the Big Waters they searched for.
Cameahwait agreed to trade twenty-nine
of his finest horses and several mules.
In exchange, Captain Clark would deliver
pistols, gunpowder, and knives on the return trip.

Of course, during the day, I assisted in the talks,
but I spent my evenings with Jumping Fish
and the other people of the village.
While I visited with my friends,
my ears were opened in the evenings
to the talk of my people.
I learned that there were many present in the tribe
who did not trust our captains,
who feared that they were in allegiance with our warring neighbors.
After all, they had just come from the Hidatsa village,
and Blackfeet Indians had been scouted by our warriors.
Perhaps the Blackfeet had made allegiance with these white men
to keep us from the buffalo hunting ground.
But, I countered, Captain Lewis has told you
that he had already received promises from the Hidatsa
that they would now be friends with the Shoshone,
and he said that he would soon secure
the same promise from the Blackfeet.

No white captain can make such a promise of a native people,
the women of the village insisted.
And why should we give the white men our valuable horses
for the meager presents of clothing, utensils, and medals?
Yes, they had given us some firearms and ammunition,
but the rest was promised only when they returned.
Who could be sure that these white soldiers would return?
No, when the appointed time came
to meet Captain Lewis with the horses,
well, then the Shoshone men would be gone on the buffalo hunt,
for this was our annual rite, and now was the time to do so.

Besides, we could not be spared so many horses.
The Blackfeet had only recently stolen a whole string of them.
Nor could our men be expected to help the captains carry
their supplies and equipment to the trail to begin their journey.
No, our people were a starving people who would better profit
from spending their time and activities
on providing for their own families.

I was alarmed.
If the Shoshone did not provide the horses,
I could not judge what the captains would do.
They were powerful with their guns,
and they would not tolerate a broken promise by our people.
Besides, it is a dishonorable thing to do—
not to honor the words spoken in the peace talks.
I felt assured that our captains were men of peace
and wished my people no harm.
The Shoshone, I was certain, would benefit
from the white man's friendship.
Their lives would be better under the rule of the White Father.
Had not my people seen how we had lived all these years
at the mercy of neighboring war tribes?

But the wives of the warriors would not listen to me,
and soon our talk was ended.
I could not speak to Cameahwait himself.
It is not the place of a squaw to tell a chief what his action must be,
even if that squaw is his sister.
Furthermore, I had lived for some years
in the camp of the enemy, the Hidatsa,
so I was not sure he would trust me.
And maybe he was not a part of this plan
to leave our captains without horses.
I did not want to accuse him and thus insult him.

So I spoke instead to Charbonneau
and insisted that he tell the captains of the plans of the Shoshone
to continue with the hunt and to withhold the horses and services.
If the peace agreements were thus abandoned by my people,
then the captains' band of men would be stranded
in a hostile land with no horses for the crossing
and no assurances of further peace with the native peoples.

Still, Charbonneau—sometimes I do not know the mind of this man—
waited for two days before he spoke to Captain Lewis
about the Shoshone warriors preparing for a hunt.
When he finally spoke, Captain Lewis was angry because of the delay.
He quickly called in Cameahwait and two of the other chiefs.
I tried to keep the emotion from my voice as I translated the words.
I feared for both my people and the captains.
I wanted these talks to go well.
Had not these chiefs promised, Captain Lewis demanded,
that they should assist with transporting his baggage
and supplies to the road of travel?
Had they not promised to arrive with horses and mules
so that his men could begin their journey?
Cameahwait remained silent for some time,
his head bent, not raising his eyes to meet Captain Lewis's.
Yes, he agreed finally, his plans for the hunt were wrong.
He had made these plans because his people were so hungry.
They are starving, he added, his voice soft but firm.
It is our time for the buffalo hunt, he insisted.
Other bands of Shoshone were already meeting with the Flatheads.
He was anxious that his own band would not be delayed.
Any loss of time would cost his people fresh buffalo meat.
But he agreed that he would honor the agreement.
His men would assist with carrying the bundles of goods,
and he would bring the promised horses.

Captain Clark declared that we must resume our travels immediately,
for snow had already appeared on the peaks of the highest mountains.

Our canoes were sunk and filled with stone.
We would retrieve them on our return trip.
The journey before us now would be on horse and foot.
Captain Lewis surprised me greatly
when he declared that I should not walk on this journey.
He and Charbonneau had traded goods with the tribesmen,
and they now presented me with a horse.
It was a splendid horse,
the color of sand with a dark mane and tail.

I could hardly believe that I would ride atop such an animal.
When we left our camp, our white men were all walking,
for the other horses were burdened with huge bundles of provisions.
I was the only one riding atop a fine horse.
I turned and waved to my Shoshone family and friends as we departed.

I wondered what they thought,
for such a thing as this is never seen—
a squaw on horseback while her husband walks behind.

CLARK

We launched our canoes on July 15,
our spirits soaring with the anticipation of being underway.
We noted abundant sunflowers in bloom
and came across great numbers of red, yellow, purple, and black currants
and also service berries, which we indulged in for a succulent snack.
I think these fruits actually preferable to the ones that grow
in our gardens back east.

The mountains loomed on all sides like a giant amphitheater,
one rung after another piled on top of each other.
The most distant were covered with snow.
They became obscured, however,
when we entered an area of towering cliffs,
which rose above the river to heights of twelve hundred feet.
We were frustrated by the many turns and bends in the river,
which prevented us from seeing what lay ahead.
Our men labored excessively, pulling the canoes.
Sometimes their feet slipped precariously.
At other times, they were cut by sharp rocks.

The great buffalo herds were now behind us.
All the big game was scarce.
More dismal—there was no whisky left,
and the days were growing shorter.

I took this part of the journey by land,
and my feet suffered from it.
Shredded by the prickly pears,
they were a mass of raw, bleeding flesh.
Mosquitoes and gnats added to our misery.
Needle grass was yet another source of torture.
This plant contained barbed seeds,
which penetrated our moccasins and leather leggings,
causing much pain until they were removed.
Lewis's dog suffered immensely.
He bit and scratched until he howled with pain.

A pervasive mood of gloom enveloped the men.
I noted, however, that one character's spirits were well aloft.
Sacagawea, normally quiet and restrained,
was increasingly animated, bubbling with an optimistic energy.
She declared a kinship with this land, asserting that we were
in the homeland of her first family, the Shoshone.
She announced that we would soon come to a place
where three forks in the river come together.

We began to see evidence of human habitation,
broken pieces of pottery left behind
and the remnants of a campfire.
I left some presents of cloth and linen
to inform the Indians that we were not enemies,
but white men who come as friends.
Sacagawea pointed out a grove of pine trees
where the bark had been stripped.
She explained that the Indians
would eat the soft underparts of the wood.

I thought that they must surely be a poor, starving people
if they resorted to such a diet.

On July 22, we came to a creek Sacagawea recognized.
It was a place where her people came to get white earth for paint.
We would be coming to the Three Forks, she assured us, very soon.
Her prediction was accurate.
The mood of the crew considerably lightened
when we came to the junction of the three rivers.
The country suddenly opened before us,
revealing a beautiful, extensive area of plain and meadow,
which remained encircled by the looming mountains.

I, unfortunately, found myself quite sick
with fever, chills, and muscle pain,
so we rested for two days at Three Forks.
The men busied themselves with hunting meat
and making and mending clothing.
Sacagawea announced that we were camped on exactly the spot
where she was captured by the Hidatsa some years past.
She recounted the story of her attack without emotion,
and we asked no further questions of her,
being respectful of the circumstances.

We came to a place where an outcropping of rock
projected itself above the barren landscape.
Sacagawea's excitement grew.
She informed us that this was indeed the hunting grounds
of her people, and we could not be far from her village.
The place was called Beaverhead Rock
for its resemblance to the head of a beaver swimming in water.

I was feeling much better at this point,
but a painful tumor appeared on my ankle,
making it difficult for me to walk.
Lewis and I agreed that he should take Drouillard

and several other men with him in search of the Shoshone,
while I, with my painful ankle, followed at a slower pace.

Lewis's party was gone for over a week,
and we grew anxious.
Finally, one morning we spotted
a band of people approaching in the distance.
As they drew nearer, we recognized the foremost figure.
It was Drouillard!
Behind him was what looked to be an entire village of Indians.
They appeared quite joyous and eager to make our acquaintance.

When Sacagawea caught sight of them,
she was overcome with emotion.
She danced and displayed the most extravagant joy.
Never in the entire period of our journey
had I seen her anything but calm and composed,
but now she abandoned herself to the rush of feelings.
She skipped ahead, looking back to me at regular intervals.
She put her fingers to her mouth,
indicating that these were her people,
the tribe that had given her nurturance as an infant.

One of the Shoshone young women,
who looked to be about the same age as Sacagawea,
broke from the crowd and ran with extended arms to Sacagawea.
The two of them exchanged shouts and words of joy.
They fervently embraced.

Sacagawea let us know that this girl
had been captured with her by the Hidatsa
but was now safely back with these, her people.
It was a touching sight.
We were moved by the ardent manner
in which they expressed their feelings
and by the sheer unusualness of the situation presented—

for two young friends to have been captured together years ago,
only to be separated and lost to each other
and then to come face to face once again in their homeland—
it was a most remarkable occurrence.

The Shoshone warriors showed no restraint when meeting us.
They quickly identified me as leader,
and I was soon assaulted
by what Lewis later termed the "national bear hug."
This maneuver involved pressing a side of their face against mine
and embracing me fiercely.
I was quite smeared with bear grease and paint.
Finding the greetings thoroughly exhausting,
I was glad when we resumed our trek to the village.

Once we arrived, I was immediately reunited with Lewis.
The two of us were ushered to a circular tent
where the Shoshone chiefs were ready to speak in council.
One of the chiefs positioned me on a white robe
and tied six white shells into my hair.
We removed our moccasins as a sign of our intention to stay the course.
The peace pipe was passed.

After smoking and exchanging pleasantries,
we sent for Sacagawea.
She entered and began the process of interpreting
when, suddenly, her facial expression underwent transformation.
And then in one great leap,
she bounded across the circle
and threw her blanket so that it was over both her head
and that of the principal chief, Chief Cameahwait.
We soon learned that he was her brother,
whom she feared had perished on the day she was taken.
With some effort, her brother finally unwrapped her arms
and insisted she resume her seat,
but she could not restrain the tears that flowed freely as she conversed.

Captain Lewis spoke to the chiefs of our good intentions
to bring peace and prosperity to the Shoshone people.
He apprised them of our desire to find the best route across the mountains
and of our immediate need of thirty or so horses to carry our goods.
He also enquired about securing a guide.

The talks were slowed by the progression of interpretation.
What Captain Lewis and I said in English
was translated in French by Labiche to Charbonneau.
Charbonneau spoke in Hidatsa to Sacagawea,
who relayed our thoughts to the Shoshone in her native language.
A complex, but necessary, process—
we were heartily thankful for our interpreters at this juncture.

We presented the Shoshone with gifts.
Cameahwait, whose name means *one who never walks,*
was the apparent head chief.
We gave him a Jefferson medal, a uniform coat,
a pair of scarlet leggings, and a carrot of tobacco.
To the lesser chiefs, we extended smaller medals with Washington's likeness,
shirts, leggings, handkerchiefs, knives, and tobacco.
And to the other Indians present,
we gave paint, awls, knives, beads, and mirrors.

When talk had concluded for the day,
we gathered outside, where Lewis shot the air gun.
The tribesmen were much impressed and excited,
pronouncing the air gun "great medicine."
They were also awed by Lewis's dog,
having never seen such a large and furry specimen.
Cameahwait invoked the Shoshone custom of honoring a new friend
and pledging mutual allegiance by giving me his own name.
The Shoshone actually called me Cameahwait
for the duration of our visit,
which I found both touching and amusing.

We spent the next few days in the company of Cameahwait.
His disposition was easy, reserved;
he spoke in a sincere manner,
imparting a good deal of information regarding
the next part of our journey.
We came to understand that the Lemhi River flowed into the Salmon,
the Salmon into the Snake,
the Snake into the Columbia,
and the Columbia into the Pacific.
Cameahwait was firm in his belief, however,
that a straight river route would be impossible,
the various rivers being mostly unnavigable.

Cameahwait let us know that the two lesser chiefs
were displeased with their gifts.
We gave them a few more of our old coats,
and Lewis promised more presents,
especially firearms and ammunition,
if they should assist with helping us cross the mountains.
Frankly, the chiefs appeared half-starved,
so we also presented them with fish, corn, beans, and dried squash.
Cameahwait pronounced the squash the best food he had ever tasted,
excepting the sugar lump given to him by Sacagawea.

I spent seven days investigating the river ways
and found that what the chiefs had told me was true.
They were lined with rugged banks and full of rapids.
Our canoes could not navigate them.
It seemed our only route would be the one by land.
While I was gone, Lewis bartered for our horses,
promising pistols, gunpowder, and knives for twenty-nine horses.

We named our campsite Camp Fortunate
for our lucky experience.
We dug pits and cached some of our supplies in the final days,
out of the sight of the Shoshone.

Likewise, we sunk our canoes and pirogues
with the intention of retrieving them on our return journey.

On August 24, as we made final preparations,
Charbonneau casually announced alarming news.
Cameahwait and his warriors were planning
a buffalo hunting expedition for the very next day.
We could hardly believe it,
for if they were going on the hunt,
then we would certainly be left high and dry,
without the Shoshone men to help transport our baggage
and, worst of all, without the horses we direly needed.
Time was of utmost importance, likewise,
for soon the mountain trails would be covered with snow.
Lewis profusely berated Charbonneau for being tardy
in relaying this information to us.
Apparently, Sacagawea had pressed him
to let her brother's plans be known some days before.

We immediately summoned Cameahwait
and several of the other chiefs.
After some talk, Cameahwait hung his head
and admitted that was indeed the plan,
adding that his people were starving,
and it was well past the time for the buffalo hunt.
Already other Shoshone bands were gathering
with the Flatheads to begin a large hunt.
To our great relief, he agreed to be a man of his word, however,
and to honor his agreement.
He would bring us the horses
and also supply men to assist with transporting our supplies.

We concluded, somewhat uneasily,
that matters were once again settled
and spent an evening in festivity,

with Cruzatte playing his fiddle.
Both our men and the Indians danced merrily.

We remained on guard, however,
ever aware of the capricious nature of the Shoshone,
which we came to understand was due to their
extreme state of poverty.
They were at the mercy of the tribes who carried guns.
The Shoshone could only hunt buffalo
by sneaking onto the plains and retreating quickly back
to their mountain hideaways.
Nor did they have a sufficiently sophisticated political system.
A chief was only a chief so long as his men chose to follow him.
Cameahwait had argued in our favor
even when the lesser chiefs and other warriors were suspicious.
I was sure he felt the burden of their grumbling and complaints
as well as the heavy responsibility for the welfare of his tribe.
Conflicted, he, no doubt, felt it his duty
to address the wishes and needs of his own people.
This we understood.

On August 30, we bid farewell to our Shoshone friends.
Swooping Eagle, called "Toby" by the traders,
agreed to go with us and serve as our guide.
We loaded our horses with packed goods.
We men would walk behind.
Captain Lewis and Charbonneau, however,
presented Sacagawea with a horse for riding.
I was glad they had extended this gift to her
because I had observed how happy she had been
here with her people, in the company of other women,
her baby coddled and cared for by all of them.
I feared that she would want to remain in her native home,
but she appeared quite agreeable to continue.

September 1805–March 1806
IDAHO TO THE PACIFIC COAST

SACAGAWEA

We traveled a straight and easy road for several days,
but then our road became a path
through dense forests of trees and brush.
Finally, it was a straight-up road with steep and rocky slopes,
where the horses' feet slipped on damp stones.
Several times our horses fell and rolled down embankments.
The men would often ask me to coax them back up
because they said the horses responded to my gentle voice.
We were fortunate that we did not lose any of them.

We met with days of rain and hail and even early snow.
The traveling was so troublesome, the men had no time to hunt.
Our supplies were limited—no flour, no meat—
only a little corn and a few dried berries remained.
The captains commanded two of our horses be killed and eaten.
The others were glad for this meat,
but I could not eat the meat of such a fine companion.

We were lucky to meet with a band
of Flathead Indians who were kind to us.
Chief Three Eagles gave us gifts of otter fur and antelope skin.
The women gave us dried roots and berries.
We purchased thirteen more horses from them.

Soon our journey was eased, but still we had
more days of climbing mountains
and falling horses and scarce game.
When we stopped and rested by a creek,
we named it Hungry Creek.

Finally, we descended what we judged
to be the farthest mountain.
We came to a deep forest and then a beautiful prairie,
where blue camas flowers peered out from swaying, green grass.
Here we saw children playing.
Native men appeared on horseback
and took us to their village.
The French traders called these people the Nez Perce
because of their pierced noses.
Their clothes bore many ornaments of beads and shells.

The Nez Perce language sounded strange to me,
unlike the language of other native tribes.
Neither I, nor our interpreters, could understand their words.
Still, the people were generous, giving us gifts
of buffalo meat, dried salmon, berries, and camas roots.

After we had rested near their village for several days,
we learned alarming news.
Several Nez Perce braves had counseled the chiefs
to kill all of our soldiers and take our possessions,
for then they would be a rich people
with cooking pots and guns and ammunition
that would last them for a generation.

But this did not happen.
No, they were dissuaded
by the words of the old grandmother, Watkuweis.
Her name means *return from a far land.*
I was anxious to meet this woman,
who spent her days lying on her bed.
She spoke to me in sign language,
revealing that she had been captured years ago
by the Blackfeet, who were cruel to her.
White traders were kind,
supplying her with food and a horse,
and she finally made her way back to her people.

When she heard her people plotting to kill our men,
she protested, "You must do them no harm.
The white people have been a good friend to me."
I shared my own story of capture and travel.
She was delighted with my son Baptiste.
With my help, she held him in her arms
and even let him chew on her fingers.
Baptiste loved to chew on fingers at this time.
His gums were swollen and sore.
When I rubbed them, I felt the hard knobs of teeth beneath.

I learned about the camas root
while we were with the Nez Perce,
for the women spent much time digging it up.
When they had a sufficient quantity,
they would dig a deep pit
and line it with split wood and stones.
A fire was lit until the stones were hot,
then the fire was put out.
The camas roots were roasted
between layers of grass placed upon the stones.
Many bulbs were cooked at one time.
When the baking was done,

they were formed into bread cakes,
which were sweet and good to eat.

The Nez Perce women also showed me another plant
called the death plant, which was to be avoided.
The bulb of this plant was poisonous.

We quickly filled our empty stomachs with camas cakes,
but many of the men ate too much at one time,
and they were gravely sick and forced
to spend seven full days at rest.

Chief Twisted Hair was happy to be our friend.
On white elk skin, he drew a map of the three rivers,
which would take us to the Big Waters.
It would be a journey of twelve days, he informed us.
Captain Lewis and Captain Clark liked Twisted Hair,
and they trusted him.
It was decided to leave our horses
in his care until we came back.
The horses were branded, and our saddles were buried.
Captain Clark traded for food for our trip.

We would need canoes, however,
for we would once again be traveling by river.
Of course, it would be an easier journey,
for we had now reached the place
where we no longer had to fight against the current.
From this point forward, the water flowed to the sea.
Our men felled two cottonwood trees.
The Nez Perce showed the men how to burn out the middle
so that the work of making canoes was much easier.

Several of the Nez Perce agreed to travel with us,
serving as our guides.
We were happy when our canoes moved swiftly,

but soon we encountered churning rapids,
and several times our canoes were overturned.
It was only with quick action
that our men were rescued and put back in the boats.

The mountain streams were filled with salmon,
but our men preferred red meat,
so when we encountered native peoples,
our captains traded for dogs,
which our men killed and roasted.
This caused me as much grief
as the eating of horses.
In my native villages, dogs were our friends.
We would never eat one of them.

Various tribes of native peoples stood along the banks
and watched as we passed.
Sometimes they beckoned to us,
inviting us to their village.
But when we first saw the Walla Walla people,
they were not friendly
but sat on horses, their weapons drawn.
When one of these braves spotted me,
he quickly pointed and spoke to the others.
They all lowered their weapons then
and approached us in a friendly manner.
Captain Clark said it was because of me
that they extended their goodwill.
My presence, he insisted, let them know
that we came as a friendly, peaceful people
because no war party ever traveled with a squaw and child.

Our journey down the river continued to be
a treacherous one with many rapids and jagged rocks.
Sometimes we had to carry
both the provisions and the boats on our backs.

When the river widened,
and clouds of fog settled in the low places,
then the days were cool without being cold.
Soft rain fell almost every day.
Our captains said they were sure
we were near the Big Waters.
Captain Clark left our camp and traveled by foot
until he came to the place
of crashing waves and roaring water.
It was a wonderful sight, he informed us.

We were visiting with the Chinook peoples at this time.
These people made use of a wapato root,
which grows in the mud of shallow waters.
I learned how to gather these roots
by standing in a stream and shifting my feet about.
When I found a wapato,
I would curve my toe and foot around it,
dislodge it, and bring it to the top.
I roasted it in embers until it was soft and agreeable to eat.
I was very glad to have these wapato roots.

In the Chinook village, Captain Lewis saw
a native man wearing a robe of sea otter skins.
Captain Lewis thought it the most beautiful fur he had ever seen.
He offered many things for this robe—
white beads, red beads, a blanket, a coat—
but the man refused his offers.
He declared he would give his robe to the captain
if he could have my belt of blue beads.
This belt had been a special gift from my Hidatsa mothers.
It had traveled a great distance with me.
I was not pleased to part with it,
but I recalled the many kindnesses of Captain Lewis,
and I agreed to this trade.

Captain Lewis received the otter skin robe,
and he gave me a warm blue coat of cloth.

Winter was upon us once again.
The captains held council to decide where
we should build a winter fort.
The captains asked that all of us vote on this matter,
even York and me, although slaves and women
are never allowed to vote in other places.
I myself voted to camp near the place
where the wapato roots grow in abundance,
but the others voted to cross to the good hunting ground
near the Clatsop Indians,
and that is where we went.
One of our men immediately killed an elk.
We ate the marrow from the two shank bones
and chopped the bones fine.
Then we boiled the bone in water and took from the liquid
a jar of grease, which Captain Clark said would oil the boots and guns.

We built a fort of seven huts
to sustain us through the winter.
It was not cold, but it was very wet.
During the passing of one full moon,
we only saw the sun three times.
The men were often sick with colds.
Tumors and boils erupted on their skin.

Still, when again it was the time of celebration
of the birth of the holy infant,
our camp was full of merriment.
The soldiers awakened our captains with the salute of shooting guns,
and there Iewas much singing.
The captains gave each man a gift of tobacco and a handkerchief.
I gave Captain Clark a present of two dozen white weasel tails.

He was much pleased with this gift,
embracing me and kissing my forehead.

Because of the warm weather, our meat spoiled quickly.
Captain Lewis declared that we could retrieve salt
from the waters of the ocean to serve as a preservative.
He sent five of our men to the coast,
where they boiled sea water and extracted the salt,
which was white and fine and very good.
We were all pleased to have salt to preserve our meat,
for much of the old meat had rotted.

At the coast, our men met native peoples
who gave them blubber from a great fish, the whale.
This blubber was good to taste.
The fish was a monstrous size, they reported,
longer than five of our canoes laid out in a line.
The captains determined that we should send
a party of men to see this fish
and to bring back some of the meat and more of the blubber.

I wanted to see the great fish;
I wanted to see the Great Waters;
I wanted to travel with the captains and our men.
But the captains said no; I should stay back at the camp
and care for Baptiste, who was now crawling about
and making a nuisance of himself.
But, I protested, Baptiste could still travel in a cradle board,
and I was strong and willing.
Besides, I had traveled a long way to see the Great Waters,
and now that there was a monstrous fish,
I wished to see it also.
I had come such a long way, I had never complained,
and I had never made a request before.
The captains, seeing my strong desire,
finally agreed—yes, I could travel with them.

Our trip to the Big Waters was a journey of five days.
The first part of our journey was on foot.
We crossed three marshes and then waded across several creeks,
where we met a native man whom Captain Clark hired
to take us to the spot where the whale lay.
We traveled some distance over slippery stone
and came to the foot of a steep hill.
It was not easy to climb this hill.
But we finally did so by pulling ourselves up over bushes and roots.
Then we continued on a bad road
through a tangle of logs and underbrush.
We camped that night in a grove of spruce and white cedar.

The next morning, we climbed to the highest point
and looked below to see the ocean.
We watched as the great waves crashed against the rock.
We made the steep, slippery descent,
knowing that if our feet slid,
we could fall to our deaths,
but we did not fall.
We safely reached the beach,
where we found what was left of the big fish,
who had been stranded on a large rock.
He was no longer a creature of flesh,
for the native peoples had removed all of it.
We saw only the great white skeleton of bones.
Still, I thought it a wondrous sight
and was glad that I had made the journey.

The Great Waters—the ocean! What a powerful force!
Fierce water with churning white waves
stretched out before us to the point where sky and water meet
and land could no longer be seen.

Charbonneau and I laughed at the sea otters,
whom I called *the water people.*

Their faces reminded me of the faces of people.
Although they loved to swim, they were not fish,
for they came out of the water and walked upon the sand.
Baptiste pointed at them and babbled.
They raised their curious heads at his remarks,
but still they would not approach
and quickly went to the water when I stepped closer.

We returned to our camp, which we called Fort Clatsop,
with buckets of blubber retrieved from the whale.
We spent three months at the fort.
In this time I helped with sewing hides
and making new clothes and moccasins.
Although it was not cold,
we were bothered much by rain and hail and thunderstorms.
We hated the sand fleas, which constantly plagued us.
I rubbed Baptiste with bear oil to keep the fleas from his skin,
but only sometimes did it help.

Spring came early.
When the elk began retreating to the mountains,
the captains judged it was time for us to begin our trip home.

September 1805–March 1806
IDAHO TO THE PACIFIC COAST

CLARK

Summer was fading quickly,
and we knew winter came early to the mountains,
so we were anxious to be on our way.
By early September, we had already encountered a hard freeze.

We were obliged to cut our way through thickets
for lack of any kind of road.
Our horses were in constant danger
of slipping on the rocky slopes.
Several of them actually did turn over
and roll down the hillside.
A large buckskin mare threw her load against a tree,
breaking our last thermometer as well as my writing desk.
The Appaloosa was crippled,
and the black horse and the roan simply gave out.

Our food supplies dwindled.
We had only a little parched corn
and were without fresh meat.

Several times our horses strayed
as they searched for grass to graze.
Looking for them cost us valuable travel time.
Our guide, Old Toby, became lost at one point.
We wasted several days dejectedly milling about.

September 16 was one of our worst days.
Snow began to fall three hours before the break of dawn
and continued throughout the day
to a depth of six to eight inches.
It was quite common for the pines, burdened with heavy snow,
to dump a load on the men who passed under them.
I myself was miserable.
In all the years I had lived,
this was the wettest and coldest I had ever felt.
The icy chill permeated every bone of my body.

There was little animal life to speak of—
pheasants here and there, small gray squirrels,
and occasionally blue vulture birds.
We were forced to kill two colts for food.
The only resources left then were our guns and packhorses.
We considered killing the horses,
but that would mean abandoning the baggage
we would need for our return trip.
Sacagawea protested the slaughter of the colts,
saying it was a barbaric thing to do.
She was angry with me when I would not halt the order.
I had the needs of my men to consider.
They had become a ragged, thin, sickly bunch.
The men, despite the dire situation, complained little.
My affection and admiration for them increased each day.

When we followed a creek to the forks,
we found a village of Flathead
with thirty-three lodges and about four hundred members.

We received a friendly welcome.
Their chiefs threw white robes over our shoulders
and insisted on smoking the peace pipe with us.

In mid-September, we were delighted
to see a large tract of prairie country in the distance.
I scouted ahead and came upon three small native boys playing.
I befriended them by giving them blue and red ribbons.
They took me to their village—a Nez Perce settlement.
The people there gave us buffalo meat, dried fish,
camas roots, and berries.

I made the acquaintance of Twisted Hair, the head chief.
I judged him to be in his mid-sixties.
He appeared to be a cheerful, sincere man.
He drew a map for us on white elk skin,
indicating the two villages in the area.
One village was close to the camas flats
where the beautiful blue and violet flowers grow.
The Indian women gathered great quantities of the root
to be prepared as a kind of bread or cake.
Twisted Hair indicated it would be a journey
of five sleeps to the Columbia River
and then one more to the falls of the Columbia.
He told me we would meet a great number of Indians
residing on the forks of the main river.
At the falls, he reassured me,
we would see an establishment of white people.

We passed medals to Twisted Hair
and three of his lesser chiefs.
We also doled out the usual number
of shirts, knives, handkerchiefs, and tobacco.
Unfortunately, the Nez Perce weren't satisfied with our trinkets,
and though they had been generous up to this point,

they were no longer willing to continue to feed our men.
We were forced to trade from our diminishing supply.

We were so starved at this point
that we overindulged in what they did give us.
Furthermore, our stomachs weren't used
to the diet of fish and roots,
and most of the men became violently ill,
unable to do much but lie about.
It was nearly a full week before we recovered.

Our friendship and trust with the Nez Perce grew, however,
and after several days, the chiefs felt free to admit
that several of their warriors had plotted to kill our party.
They held in their possession only two inferior rifles,
and they were constantly harassed by their neighbors, the Blackfeet.
They could have lived well with our arsenal of weapons for many years.

But they were dissuaded by an old woman named Watkuweis,
whose name translates as *returned from a far country*.
She had been captured some years earlier by Blackfeet,
who had treated her harshly.
Befriended by white traders,
she eventually made her way back to her people.
When she learned of our presence,
she called all of the chiefs and head men to her dwelling,
for she was old and too unwell to venture out.
She repeated the stories of her life,
explaining how she had survived
only by the generous spirit of the white men.
She insisted that no harm be done to any white person.
Sacagawea was drawn to her because of their similar circumstances.
She and Pomp spent many hours in Watkuweis's lodge.

I noted that both Sacagawea and Pomp fared well during this time.
I attributed this to the fact that Sacagawea

had been raised on a native diet.
The camas roots, no doubt, provided nourishment for her,
even though it was such a source of pain and discomfort for us.

As soon as the men had recovered,
we set about the business of making canoes.
We were grateful to the Nez Perce
for sharing their tricks of the trade.
Instead of spending hours chopping out trees,
their method was to utilize a slow-burning fire,
which hollowed out the center of the canoe.
After ten days, we had accomplished our task,
producing four large canoes and one small one.

Twisted Hair promised to look after
our herd of horses until our return.
We loaded our canoes and set them in the river on October 6.
We made twenty miles that first day,
but then came upon a bad stretch of rapids,
which I thought to portage around.
Captain Lewis was determined, though,
to shoot down the rapids.
When he succeeded, the rest of us followed.
Old Toby was so frightened by this running of the rapids
that he quickly and quietly abandoned us.

Of course, the going was rough on our canoes.
They frequently overturned or grounded on rocks.
Sometimes they swamped; other times they leaked.
We were determined to run the rapids anyway,
as many as fifteen in a day.
We lost supplies and damaged some of our trade goods.
Looking back, I realize we were reckless
to the point of putting our men's lives in danger,
such was our drive at this point to finally reach our destination.

When we reached the Snake River, we camped
and bought dogs and dried fish from a local Indian tribe.
The river teemed with salmon,
but we sorely missed our diet of fresh meat.
I enjoyed an especially good dinner when I shot a blue-winged teal.

Proceeding toward the junction of the Snake and the Columbia,
we passed through a new terrain where canyons lined the river.
It was common to see Indians watching us from the bank.
On one occasion, we met a party of Walla Wallas,
who appeared quite unfriendly.
We endured a few tense moments
until they spotted Sacagawea with Pomp,
at which point they were immediately at ease.
Captain Lewis and I both counted ourselves lucky
then that she was with us.
Her presence was a constant reassurance
to the native peoples that we came in peace,
for no warring people would ever travel
with a woman and a baby.

On October 11, we stopped to trade with a band of Nez Perce.
We purchased a fair amount of salmon and also seven dogs.
Here we observed a novel kind of vapor bath or sweat house,
different than we had seen with other tribes.
The bath consisted of a hollowed square, six to eight feet deep,
with only a two-foot opening at the top.
The bathers descended through the hole,
bringing with them heated stones and jugs of water.
They threw the water on the stones to produce a steam.
Here they sat until they deemed they had perspired sufficiently,
their bodies cleansed and purified.
Then they plunged into the cold water of the nearby stream.

At times, we found various Indians to be troublesome
on this stretch of the journey;

not that we felt physically threatened to the point of death,
but rather they were inclined to indulge in petty thievery,
robbing us of food, wood, cooking instruments.
My own impatience mounted when I discovered
that my pipe tomahawk had been stolen.
I even saw one of the tribesmen smoking with it.
Drouillard was grieved when his capote,
a heavy, hooded blanket coat, was stolen.
At one point, the men's tolerance had reached its limit,
and I heard mutterings of killing one of the thieves.
I wasn't sure if they were serious or not,
but I felt obliged to remind them that it was absolutely necessary
to ingratiate ourselves to the Indians
so that we could count on a friendly reception on our return trip.

Proceeding onward, we watched as tawny grasses
gave way to green forests.
On October 31, we came upon a remarkable detached rock
that stood about eight hundred feet in height.
I judged it would take four hundred paces to get around it.
We named it Beacon Rock.
Surveying the river at this juncture,
I observed that it gave every appearance
of being affected by the tide.
All signs told me we were nearing the ocean.

On November 4, a mountain came into view.
Covered with snow, it resembled a sugarloaf.
The days were rainy and cloudy,
the fog often so thick we could not see
the opposite shore of the river.

On November 5, we met a flotilla of coastal canoes.
I was impressed with the design and construction.
A bear's image was carved into the bow,
and a man's image was on the stern.

The next day another flotilla arrived with roots, trout, and furs.
We were pleased at the reasonable costs,
which were unlike the outrageously high prices
we had encountered with other tribes.
I bought two beaver skins for a mere five fishhooks.

November 7 dawned with the typical fog.
We set about when it had partially lifted.
By midafternoon, the sky had cleared.
I caught my first glimpse of the Pacific Ocean
and joyfully shouted, "Ocean in view. O! The joy!"
We paddled on in a near state of ecstasy.
The winds, however, soon brought us back
to the reality of our full circumstances,
for they were maddening, and the rain prevailed.

On November 17, I took a party overland
and viewed the vastness of the Pacific.
Standing on a high promontory,
I reflected on the absurdity of this ocean's name,
for it was by no means peaceful or *pacific*.
No, this ocean was a mass of rollicking water,
which produced a thunderous roar
as giant waves crashed against the rugged boulders.

Captain Lewis, meanwhile, had set off in a different direction,
where he had unfortunate experiences with the Chinook Indians.
When he sent Privates Shannon and Willard on a hunting expedition,
they spent the night with five Chinooks.
In the middle of the night, the Indians stole their rifles.
Lewis arrived with his party the next morning.
Making threatening gestures,
he persuaded the braves to return the guns.
Shannon took the errant Indians into custody
and marched them to my camp.
I was outraged upon learning of their behavior

and promised that I would shoot them
if anything at all should ever be found missing from our possession.

When I met up with Captain Lewis several days later,
he was in the company of a band of Chinooks,
who were, thankfully, a peaceful element of the tribe.
Several of them were chiefs.
We smoked with them and handed out medals and a flag.
One of the chiefs had a robe of sea otter skins.
I proclaimed it the most beautiful thing I had ever seen.
Lewis sorely wanted it, and he offered a watch, a handkerchief,
a dollar, and a bunch of red beads.
The chief flatly refused each offer.
What he wanted the most was
Sacagawea's belt of blue beads.
Of course, I was sure this chief could not have it,
for I knew how much the belt meant to her.
It had been given to her by her adoptive mothers
to honor her hard work and loyalty,
and she had worn it with pride and cherished it for several years now.
To my surprise, however, she agreed to trade.
We rewarded her with one of our own coats of heavy, blue cloth.

We sent out scouting parties in hopes of finding trading vessels
anchored at the mouth of the Columbia,
but our spirits sank when none were found.
We had hoped that we could use Jefferson's letter of credit
to obtain ample trading goods for our return trip.
We also had hoped to send a copy of our journals
back to Jefferson at this point,
in the event that neither we nor our possessions survived.
I think we partly hoped that we could make the return trip
by way of sea ship, perhaps one even sent by Jefferson,
but those thoughts collapsed when none were sighted.

I took a moment to reflect on the physical condition
of the men at this point.
We were a sorrowful sight.
Our clothes and coats were rags.
Our leather garments and attachments had rotted.
The men were thin and sickly.

We determined then we would have to winter on the coast.
On November 24, Lewis and I decided
to put the matter of where to make our camp to a vote.
Everyone, including my slave York and Sacagawea, had a say.
Sacagawea made her plea in the most earnest and delightful manner.
She reminded us that we had nearly starved not long ago.
We should, therefore, camp in a place that assured abundant food.
The best place would be nearby fields
where plants and roots flourished.
Others offered their observations of nearby sites.
After some discussion, we chose a high spot above the coastal marshes.
We would be protected there by a grove of pine trees.
The Clatsop tribe, whom we found quite agreeable,
would be our immediate neighbors.

We set about building a fort with cabins and a stockade.
The Clatsop were amused and stopped to watch our progress,
bringing gifts of berries and roots.
We judged them to be the best groomed
and cleanest tribe of people we had met thus far.
They bathed and washed their hands frequently.
We named our camp Fort Clatsop in tribute to our neighbors.

The warm temperatures were agreeable,
but we found the constant rain very disagreeable.
Our men would bring in elk or deer,
but it would have to be eaten quickly for fear of spoiling.
Sacagawea showed me a piece of real bread,
made from flour that she had saved for Pomp.

She insisted that I take it, however,
claiming that he could not be trusted to chew it sufficiently,
that he would choke if she gave it to him.
I readily accepted, enjoying the texture and sweet taste.
Only after the last swallow did it occur to me
that I should have insisted that she eat it herself.

Pomp showed himself to be quite vigorous and lively during this time.
He quickly mastered the art of walking.
We delighted in watching his first, halting steps.
He would swing one leg forward then shift his stance and balance
before venturing to bring the opposite leg into position.
The first few days he attempted only three or four steps
and then quickly sat down with a definitive plop of his rear quarters.
But by the fourth day, he was toddling about,
gesturing to the squirrels and birds who ventured into his territory.

Christmas Day dawned gray and rainy.
The men woke us with a gun salute outside our window.
This was followed by the singing of carols.
We were soon in a festive mood.
Handkerchiefs and tobacco were passed around.
Sacagawea and Charbonneau presented me
with two dozen white weasel tails,
showing me how they could be affixed to my jacket.
I thought them a true treasure and was moved by their gesture.

Although we had included Sacagawea
in our presentation of gifts to Charbonneau,
I would have liked to have given her something
that demonstrated our gratitude
and the special affection I held for her in my heart.
I did not have anything fitting, however,
nor did I think it wise to provoke
any ill feelings from Charbonneau.

In the days that followed,
we made profitable use of our time and location.
The men set up a primitive salt works near the coast,
where they boiled seawater and retained the salt.
We used this salt to preserve our meat.
The men spent considerable time mending their clothes.
They also made new apparel from our supply of hides.

We befriended a nearby Tillamook tribe,
who gave us whale blubber.
We thought it delicious,
even better than the fatty beaver tail.
The Tillamook described a whale
that had recently washed upon the beach.
I immediately organized a party to travel to the coast
in the hope of retrieving more of the blubber and some of the meat.
I was taken aback when Sacagawea insisted
that she be allowed to travel with us.
Of course, my immediate reaction was to say *no*,
for I knew how difficult the journey to the coast would be.
But she spoke up quite clearly and distinctly,
insisting that she had traveled a long way
to see these great waters.
And now that a monstrous fish had been spotted,
she wished to see it also.
She thought it very unreasonable
that she not be allowed to accompany us.
I found that I could not deny her.

So off we went with Sacagawea and young Baptiste.
It was a most difficult trip.
We had to abandon our canoes early because of the high winds.
We waded through several creeks and marshes
and then were forced to climb a rocky cliff.
At times, we were nearly vertical.
The descent was just as perilous,

for the slope consisted of slippery clay
with a rugged rock that projected out in midair.
We were quite relieved when we stepped
onto the sandy soil at the base of the cliff.

Unfortunately, however,
by the time we reached the whale,
only a skeleton was left.
But a monstrous skeleton it was!
I estimated it to be over a hundred feet long.
The Indians were plundering what could be used.
I put my bartering skills to good use,
and we returned with three hundred pounds of blubber
and a few gallons of the rendered oil.

We remained for three long months at Fort Clatsop,
still hoping every day to see a ship coming in from the sea.
Captain Lewis spent long hours working on his journals,
which included detailed descriptions of plant and animal life
and also written sketches of the various Indian tribes.
I worked on the process of mapmaking,
carefully detailing the land from Fort Mandan to Fort Clatsop.
True, we had not found the Great Northwest Passage,
which would provide easy passage to the Pacific, but now we knew—
such a passage did not exist.
For my part, I was satisfied that I had mapped
the most practical and navigable route
across the continent of North America.

The rain came unabated through January, February, and March.
Sand fleas and biting insects tormented us.
When finally we were ready to leave,
we realized we needed one more canoe.
The Clatsops were a tough bargaining unit,
and we could not meet their price.
Out of desperation, Lewis sent four men

to steal one of their canoes,
justifying it by pointing out
that the Clatsop had stolen elk meat earlier.
When our men returned with a canoe,
unfortunately, Chief Coboway was visiting the fort,
so we quickly hid the canoe.
We took the opportunity to praise Coboway.
Lewis presented him with a certificate
noting his good conduct and helpfulness.
When he returned to our fort on March 22,
we gave him our houses and our furniture.

We pushed off on March 23,
eager to commence and complete our return journey.

PART 7—RETURN TRIP

March–August 1806
PACIFIC COAST TO NORTH DAKOTA

SACAGAWEA

As we traveled inland, the soldiers hunted again.
We ate meat of geese, ducks, and sturgeon,
but it was not enough,
so when we met with native peoples,
the men once again bought dogs.
Still I would not eat dog,
and when I watched the others,
my stomach wrenched and my heart ached.

Many native peoples by then had heard
of our presence and our mission,
and they were often eager to meet us.
We came upon bad people, though,
who tried to steal things from us—rifles, kettles, horses.
Captain Lewis was greatly distressed
when Seaman, his great black dog, was stolen.
He sent men out with instructions
to find these thieves and to fight until they got his dog back.
From this moment on, he declared, if anyone should be seen

115

with our possessions, then they should be shot.
I have never seen Captain Lewis so angry.
Seaman had been a good friend to all of us on our journey.
He had saved us from stampeding buffalo.
He had fought off charging grizzly bears.

The robber braves fled when our men caught up to them,
and Seaman was happy to travel back to his master.
The next day, the chief of these people came to apologize.
He was ashamed of the actions of his men.
His people were not usually a troublesome people.

When we reached the land of the Walla Walla people again,
Chief Yellept insisted we rest for several days.
I was glad of this time, for living with them was a Shoshone woman.
She and I spent happy times together,
recalling our early lives in Shoshone villages.
We spoke of the joy of seeing newborn colts,
of finding thick patches of wild berries,
of harvesting the meat and hides from the buffalo hunts.
We were called to interpret in the council meeting,
where Captain Lewis repeated the promises of the White Father.
Chief Yellept was fond of our captains.
He presented Captain Clark with a beautiful white horse,
and Captain Clark gave him his sword.

After we left and had traveled for a full day,
we were surprised to see three Walla Walla braves pursuing us.
When they caught up to us,
they presented us with a steel animal trap
left by one of our men on the trail.
The Walla Wallas knew that we would miss it,
and they were happy to return it to us.
Captain Lewis declared that these people, the Walla Walla,
were the best people he had met in his travels.
They were kind and helpful and worthy of our trust.

We were happy then to return to the villages of the Nez Perce.
They had proved their friendship during our past stay.
Now, when they learned that we were hungry,
they brought us baskets of dried roots and salmon.
At first, the horses we had left in their care could not be found, however.
It took several days and much arguing among the chiefs
before they were located,
but they were finally gathered and returned to us.

We rested in the Nez Perce camp for a full month.
Our men hunted and butchered and dried meat.
When several of them became sick with pains in the stomach,
I gathered a great deal of fennel root.
Captain Clark informed me that the taste is similar
 to the carrot he eats in Missouri.
The men thought the fennel delicious,
and they soon were feeling better.
Also, I found onions in abundance, and we boiled them with our meat.
Captain Clark assured me that these onions
were always good medicine for his men.

Many native travelers and hunters stopped
to visit and talk with us.
A Shoshone brave came one day with alarming words.
There was an evil, old man who was determined
to spread untrue stories about us.
He told many people that the white strangers
intended to kill the Nez Perce.

In one of the Nez Perce villages,
we found a Shoshone boy,
who was now a prisoner of the Nez Perce.
He agreed to sit in council with the chiefs and warriors
and help with interpreting.
Captain Clark and Captain Lewis
explained more about their purpose

to bring peace and prosperity to the native tribes.
They promised that trading posts would be established
where goods could be exchanged.
We went through our usual chain of interpretation—
from English to French to Hidatsa to Shoshone.
The Shoshone boy then translated to Nez Perce.

This would have been a happy time for me
except that my Baptiste became gravely ill.
He was normally such a cheerful child,
toddling behind the men as they worked,
imitating their actions.
In the evenings, he loved to dance
when Cruzatte played on his fiddle.
But one afternoon after his nap,
he did not get up from his elk hide.
Instead he whimpered and cried
and wanted nothing to eat.
I continued to nurse him, but when his bowels moved,
they produced a liquid with a vile stench.

Captain Clark gave him medicine—cream of tartar and sulphur.
He placed a poultice of wild onion around his neck,
but still Baptiste was no better.
He continued to lie on the elk hide.
Soon he was so weak, he could not even whimper.
His flesh shrunk, revealing his bones.
His face resembled the face of an old man.
Captain Clark continued to attend to him,
massaging his neck with salve of pine resin, beeswax, and bear oil.
The men thought he would not survive this illness.
Of course, they did not tell me this,
but I knew their thoughts because they no longer came
to pat his head or give words of encouragement.

Each morning I left our teepee and went to the meadow,
where I faced the rising sun and sang a prayer.
I asked that my son be restored to the child he was before.
Each morning and evening, Charbonneau held
in his hands the necklace of beads with a cross.
He prayed to the Virgin Mother, the mother of us all,
asking her to come and be with our child
and to deliver him from this sickness.
Finally, after eighteen days of sickness, Baptiste sat up.
Captain Clark declared, "Ah, Janey, our dancing boy is back!"

Our men enjoyed games and foot races with the Nez Perce
while we waited for the snows to melt.
When the blue flowers of the camas plant
bloomed on the prairie again,
we began our trek across the mountains.
Each time we reached a meadow,
we stopped to let our horses graze.
But as we traveled upward, our view changed
from flowers to pine forests,
and soon we were traveling in snow that reached the horses' flanks.
When finally we had passed the Bitterroot Mountains,
we rested at a creek that we named Traveler's Rest.
Captain Lewis and Captain Clark decided that our group should split.
We would travel different routes to gain more knowledge
of the land and various peoples.
Captain Lewis would explore the Marias River
while Captain Clark would proceed to the Three Forks
and then head to the Yellowstone River.

For this return trip, Captain Clark determined
that we should travel the road of the Flathead Indians.
We were told it was a better, shorter road
than the one we had used before.
But when we came to a wide plain,
the tracks of the native people scattered.

Captain Clark could not determine the correct trail to follow.
He wanted to go the way of Flathead Pass, but I knew this land.
I had been there often as a child.
It was a favorite place of my people
for gathering camas and other roots
and for taking beaver from the many creeks.
If we proceeded to the higher part of the plain, I informed him,
we would see a gap in the mountains
through which we could easily pass.
Captain Clark heeded my words and was pleased that he had done so.

Soon we came upon the three forks in the river,
where we had stored baggage and supplies.
The soldiers' first thought was the chewing tobacco,
for which the men had greatly longed.
They ran to the cave to find their treasure
and were delighted to chew again.

After our stop at the three forks of the Missouri,
I again showed Captain Clark a mountain pass
that would shorten our travel.
The land was rocky, so we made moccasins
for the feet of the horses.
Still, by the time we reached the Yellowstone River,
our horses' feet were very sore.
We rode for two more days
until we came to a rock that seemed to touch the sky.
We walked around it and decided
that only one side could be climbed,
for the other side was a straight cliff.
Captain Clark eagerly scaled this rock.
He reported that he saw many carvings of animals and native life.
He added his own carving with his name and the date—
Wm Clark July 25, 1806.
He declared that the rock would be called Pompy's Pillar,
in honor of my son, Jean Baptiste.

We traveled on and saw great herds of buffalo crossing the water.
Sometimes we had to stop and wait half a day to let them pass.
Many elk were in this land also.
In the evening, we heard wolves barking.
During the day, we sighted grizzly bears and ugly rattlesnakes.

We rested at the place where the two rivers,
the Yellowstone and the Missouri, meet.
But this was the resting spot
of the worst monsters of all—the mosquitoes.
We could not escape them.
They pierced through the skin of our tents.
Every night Captain Lewis's dog howled in distress.
The swarms were so great that our hunters
could not even hold one eye open to shoot from their guns.
When Captain Clark tried to shoot a bighorn sheep,
there were too may mosquitoes
on the barrel of his gun to take aim.
I smoothed bear grease on Baptiste's face,
but still he was tortured by many bites.
His face swelled so that it was twice its size.
We moved our camp further down the river,
but the mosquitoes followed us.
Finally, we were delivered from these pests
when a cold and powerful wind
arrived and blew them far from us.

The days that followed were happy ones.
Our men found antelope and deer.
I showed Captain Clark the cherries that grew on low bushes.
He liked their sweet taste and declared they were finer
than the cherries he ate back home.
Also, we dug roots of white apple, which I boiled for the men.
We ate them with our meat.
We also found gooseberries and purple berries.

During these last days of fair weather,
we reunited with Captain Lewis and his men.
They had endured many troubles during their travels.
Captain Lewis had been shot.
The ball pierced the flesh of his left thigh and grazed his right.
He was so weak that he could do little more than lie in the boat.
The accident occurred because Cruzatte, who had only one eye,
mistook our captain for an elk.
Captain Clark attended Captain Lewis,
dressing his wounds and insisting that he rest.
Captain Lewis spoke then of other dangers.
Four of his men had spent a pleasant evening
talking and smoking with the Blackfeet.
But when they awoke, they saw the native men stealing their guns.
There was fighting, and two of the Blackfeet were killed.
Captain Lewis and his men fled the camp
and were much relieved to join us again.

We made haste to be on our way,
for fear that the Blackfeet would strike back at us.
So we did not stop at the Shoshone village of my people,
but I vowed that I would return again some day
and spend pleasant days with Jumping Fish
and my adopted son, the son of my sister.

It was then a journey of only five days
before we were once again back to our home in the Mandan village,
where Charbonneau and I had lived with Otter Woman;
where we had first met Captain Clark and Captain Lewis;
where Charbonneau had signed the papers,
agreeing to serve as interpreter;
where I had given birth to Jean Baptiste.

As our canoes sailed into the village,
great crowds of people gathered on the banks.
The captains ordered that we salute them

with shots from the blunderbuss.
We stepped on land at the village of Chief Big White.
There we made our camp.
Captain Clark smoked and ate with the great chief.

Over the next few days, great numbers of native people
came to speak words with our captains
and to exchange robes and skins.
Many brought baskets of corn as gifts.
Soon we had so much corn, our canoes could not hold any more.

Captain Lewis was still weak,
so the talks and the smoking of the peace pipe
were left to Captain Clark,
and I once again assisted with interpreting.
Captain Clark issued an invitation to the chiefs.
He would be pleased if they would travel with him
to the home of the Great Father in the East.
Several of the chiefs expressed their fears.
They did not wish to leave their people at this time.
Warring tribes had recently killed
several young braves and stolen horses,
but Big White agreed to make the journey with his wife and son.

Captain Clark extended an invitation to Charbonneau and me also.
He wanted us to accompany him with Baptiste to his home,
where we would live and work near his family.
But Charbonneau informed him that he could not be useful there.
He knew no one in the United States,
and he could not make a living hunting and trapping in civilized lands.
He wished to remain in the Mandan-Hidatsa village.
I was happy with Charbonneau's decision,
for I did not want to go to the White Father's land either.
I had family and friends in the Hidatsa villages,
and I had visions of making trips to visit my Shoshone family.

Captain Clark was very sad when he heard our thoughts.
He would like to adopt Baptiste, he told us.
He is such a beautiful, promising child, he insisted.
If he, Captain Clark, were allowed to take him to his home in St. Louis,
then he would make sure that Baptiste was given
the proper upbringing and education.
This life of travel with an Indian mother and
a father who often left home to hunt and trap—
this would not be a good life for Baptiste.

But NO! We loved Captain Clark, but we loved our child much more.
We could not do this.
Charbonneau informed Captain Clark
that the child was not yet weaned
and could not be without his mother.
When he was an older child,
then we would think about bringing him
to Captain Clark's home in St. Louis.

So we said a sad farewell to Captain Clark,
and Charbonneau received his pay of $500.33.
We watched with heavy hearts
as our white friends boarded their sailing vessels
and traveled down the river.
I knew that I would not see many of these friends again.
Baptiste was distressed too, watching with sad, round eyes,
as the men waved and disappeared into the mist.

The men had been gone for only seven days
when a canoe of travelers arrived.
One of the men came forward with words on paper,
written by Captain Clark, addressed to us.
Captain Clark's letter asked us to think once more
on the plan he had presented.
He said that he had been with us a long time,
and he was glad to have gained our friendship.

He thought that I, Sacagawea, deserved a greater reward
than his government could pay me
because I had traveled the long and dangerous journey
to the Pacific and back.
And our son Pomp—he had such great fondness for him.
He was anxious to take and raise him as his own child.

If we would go to St. Louis,
he would give Charbonneau a piece of land
and horses, cows, and hogs.
We could farm this land, and he, Captain Clark,
would take charge of Pomp's education.
Or if Charbonneau did not wish to farm,
then he could find work for him as interpreter with the army.
Or perhaps Charbonneau would prefer a trading position.
He would assist Charbonneau with merchandise
and become a part of this enterprise with him.
Whichever offer Charbonneau should choose,
it would be best to bring Baptiste and me
as soon as possible.

But still our answer was the same.
We would stay here where Charbonneau would hunt and trade furs,
and Baptiste would be with me, his mother.
We stayed in the Mandan-Hidatsa village for three years.
Baptiste was no longer a baby then, but a fine little boy
who loved to follow his father about
and play hunting games with the other children.

PART 7—RETURN TRIP

March–August 1806
PACIFIC COAST TO NORTH DAKOTA

CLARK

We said our adieus on March 23.
Traveling the Columbia was hard work
as we were traveling against the strong current this time.
The water was much higher too,
because of heavy spring rains and melting snow.
Many times, we towed the canoe by hand.
As before, we encountered numerous waterfalls,
which we had to portage.
When high winds and the fierce current overtook us,
we lost one of our canoes and were forced to watch helpless
as it drifted downriver.

The Indian peoples had heard of our travels,
and now they greeted us at every turn.
Unfortunately, we also encountered
the disagreeable elements of the tribes
and found ourselves constantly on alert.
On various occasions, braves tried to steal
an ax, a kettle, food, and supplies.

Private Coulter found himself
in a man-to-man conflict for his own tomahawk.
He retained it.

Perhaps the gravest theft occurred
when Lewis's dog Seaman was stolen by three braves.
We all went into action to recover our companion.
Lewis immediately dispatched three of our men to apprehend them.
He declared that they should not hesitate to fire their guns
if they met with any resistance.
The thieves were wise enough to let Seaman go
when they realized they were being pursued.

On April 24, we resumed our march overland.
Our men suffered greatly,
complaining of soreness in their feet and legs.
When we reached the village of Chief Yellept of the Walla Wallas,
we agreed to rest and spend a few days with him,
as we had promised we would the previous October.
He supplied us with wood, dried roots, and smoked fish
when he saw how hungry we were.

On the second day of our visit,
Yellept presented me with an excellent white horse
but then indicated that he would very much like an iron kettle.
I didn't feel we could afford to hand one over.
I did part with my sword, however,
and a hundred balls and powder.
Chief Yellept seemed pleased enough with the exchange.

We were lucky to meet a captive Shoshone woman
who lived in the village.
She readily conversed with Sacagawea,
and we learned of shortcuts and easier routes to our destinations.

The Walla Wallas held a dance in our honor.
Many of the relatives and neighbors from nearby villages attended,
the number swelling to some 350 men, women, and children
as the evening progressed.
When Cruzatte broke out his fiddle,
we were amused to see that all of them sang and danced at once,
jumping up and down to the beat of the music.
Some of our men joined the dance.
We were especially delighted when Jean Baptiste,
my little boy Pomp, raised his short legs and bobbed up and down,
all the while smiling and extending his arms above his head.
He did so until he fell exhausted into his mother's arms.

On the fifth day, two of the lesser chiefs presented
both Lewis and me with a horse.
We felt moved to offer a comparable present in return.
Lewis gave them one of his own personal pistols
and several hundred rounds of ammunition.

We took leave of the Walla Wallas the following day,
declaring that they were the most friendly and honest
people we had met on our journey.
We were only out for two days
when three young Walla Walla boys rode into camp
with a trap we had negligently left behind.

We traveled on by foot for two more days,
through rain, hail, snow, and very high winds.
We were well pleased when we arrived in Nez Perce land again,
but we were short of provisions and had little left to trade.
We found that the Nez Perce were happy
to accept our medical ministrations in payment for food.
I had previously attended to an old man's worn knee and thigh,
very ceremoniously washing them and then rubbing with liniment.
Although the man had been lame for months,
he recovered enough to walk.

Word had since spread, and the Indians were all convinced
of my virtues as medicine man.
During my weeks there, I often treated forty Indians in one day.

I likewise had much success with one of our own men.
Bratton had been suffering with a bad back for a long period now.
We constructed a sweat bath lodge for him.
Stones were heated and placed inside.
Bratton entered naked with a bowl of water.
He sprinkled the stones to make them steam.
After twenty minutes, he emerged
and then plunged into cold water.
Then back to the sweat lodge he went.
Within a day, he was walking, seemingly free of pain.

We tried a similar therapy on one of the old chiefs
who was nearly paralyzed (although we did forego the cold stream).
We built a narrow lodge for him where we placed the hot stones.
We administered thirty drops of laudanum, then sent him in.
The treatment proved a great success.
He first regained the use of his hands and arms,
then also his legs and toes.

We were not so good with our own little Pomp, however.
He was in much distress from teething.
His neck and throat were swollen; his fever was high.
I gave him both tartar and sulphur.
A poultice of boiled onions was placed on his neck.
It did no good.
After several nights of much anguish,
Lewis administered a dose of cream of tartar
and reapplied a poultice of onion.
Finally, we saw a positive response.
We all gathered around him then,
softly cheering our child
and congratulating him on his reclaimed health.

Sacagawea had remained quiet and withdrawn during his illness,
but she radiated joy when Baptiste sat up again,
his eyes clear, bright, and inquisitive.

The Nez Perce persuaded us to stay for over a month,
for the Bitterroot Mountains were yet deep in snow,
and no passage could be possible until early June.
When we met up with Twisted Hair,
who had previously secured our horses,
we learned that there had been an argument
between him and Chief Cut Nose.

Fortunately, a Shoshone boy was a captive in the area.
He and Sacagawea were called in to converse with the chiefs
and help us better understand the conflict.
The boy refused to do so,
asserting that a quarrel between two chiefs was none of his business.
We gathered from the conversation, however,
that Cut Nose considered himself the greater chief.
He insisted that Twisted Hair had acted with no proper authority
when he had made the agreement to guard our horses.
Furthermore, we learned that Twisted Hair
had idly let the men ride and misuse our horses.
Many of them had been left to wander off.
When called upon, Twisted Hair could not produce them.
We were fortunate to learn that most
of them were in Broken Arm's camp.
Proceeding there, we were able to collect twenty-one horses
and about half of our saddles.

We discovered that there had been talk among the people
that we were actually bad white men
who came with the intention of killing and wiping out the Nez Perce.
Taking advantage of the Shoshone boy and Sacagawea as interpreters,
we ordered a conference to be held with all of the leading men.
We reassured them of our desire to bring peace.

We promised that we could bring prosperity to their nation,
if only they would move to the buffalo side of the mountains,
thus avoiding conflicts with the other tribes.
We also appealed to them to provide us
with guides to the Blackfoot country.
We concluded our talks with a show of our "magic,"
displaying for them a magnet, a spy glass, a compass, and a watch.
Lewis shot the air gun.
The Nez Perce were astonished and marveled at our display.

After consulting with other chiefs,
Broken Arm announced that they were ready
to do as we had requested.
He made a dish of roots and soup.
He gave a speech to his people,
asking for those who agreed with the decision
to come forward and eat.
All of them did so; there was not a dissenting voice.

Nevertheless, we learned the next day
that they would only be ready to move east of the mountains
only after the United States built a fort on the Missouri
so they could trade for arms and ammunition.

The men of the corps took advantage
of our respite with the Nez Perce,
becoming rather unhurried and sluggish,
so I was heartily glad to see them restored to activity
by engaging in sport with the Indians.
Captain Lewis and I enjoyed watching shooting matches,
horse races, foot races, and a game called prison base,
where each side took prisoners
from those who run out of the base area.
The braves and corpsmen also played a pitching game
where flattened rings were thrown at a pin.

It was a very pleasant interlude.
The memories will stay with me forever,
for it was an extraordinary sight to see both red and white men
racing over the beautiful valley,
the snow-capped mountains looming in the distance,
while crowds of onlookers cheered from the sides.
The braves gained our deepest admiration during the horse races,
for they were highly skilled horsemen.
Their horses were handsome,
with beautiful coats and graceful statures.
I favored the Appaloosa with its varied colors and spotted patterns.
The Indians took care to selectively breed these animals.

By early June, however, despite the Nez Perce's advisement
of waiting until July, we found we could wait no longer.
We set out for the Weippe Prairie.
There we dined once again on the camas roots,
which our stomachs found more tolerable this time.
In fact, we found them quite agreeable.

We had not traveled far, however,
when we found the Nez Perce's predictions to be accurate,
for we were soon enveloped in snow twelve to fifteen feet deep.
We made a camp and sent our hunters out.
Fortunately, they returned with eight deer and three bears,
so we knew we wouldn't starve.
Three young Nez Perce had agreed
to travel with us and lead us to the Great Falls.
We found them invaluable.
When we became discouraged
and felt the horses could no longer proceed without food,
the Nez Perce braves remained confident and promised
that we would soon come to grass in abundance.
We were both grateful and relieved when we did.

We enjoyed an agreeable interval when we came upon a large spring.
The Indians had formed a bath there
by stopping the run with stones and pebbles.
The water was the hottest water
I had ever encountered in the wilds of nature.
We all indulged ourselves.
The longest we could stay in the pool was nineteen minutes.

We rested near a creek at a place we called Travelers' Rest.
Here Lewis and I talked through the plans we had made earlier
when we were in Fort Clatsop.
We had decided then to break the group at this point,
Lewis taking one party and me the other,
so that we could better explore areas
that we had not explored on our forward journey.

Lewis would continue with the Nez Perce guides
to the Great Falls, traveling by a new and shorter route.
There he would explore the area north of the Missouri.
My group, with Charbonneau and Sacagawea,
would travel south through the mountains to Three Forks,
then we would head east to the Yellowstone.
We expected to encounter Crow Indians in our travels
and knew that Sacagawea would be helpful as interpreter
because the Crow language was so similar to the Hidatsa.
Our proposed rendezvous point was
a full five hundred miles east of our parting point.
It was a complex plan,
involving travel into dangerous Indian territory,
but Lewis felt strongly that we should take every opportunity
to acquire more information about the land
and make every conceivable effort to broker peace
among the various tribes, so we parted.
The first days of travel proceeded pleasantly enough
for we saw numerous beavers, otters, deer,
antelope, and bighorn sheep on the higher slopes.

When we came to a crossing point, however,
I was in agony about which direction to take.
Sacagawea asserted that she knew the land well,
that her people had gathered roots here many times.
She recommended traveling through a gap in the mountains
rather than over the trail we had utilized previously.
The new route would take us to Camp Fortunate,
where we had buried our goods earlier for safekeeping.
To my delight, she was exactly right.
We retrieved the canoes we had buried
and even the chewing tobacco we had hidden in a cave.
This heartened our men to a considerable degree.

As we proceeded to the Yellowstone, mountains rose before us.
We noticed two roads, each leading to a different pass.
Once again, I was conflicted.
I favored the northerly pass,
but Sacagawea insisted that the southern pass was by far the best.
Her advice proved invaluable on this occasion as well,
and our journey was considerably shortened.
When we reached the Yellowstone,
we built small, hide-covered canoes,
which took us down the currents.

We were dismayed one morning to learn
that we had lost twenty-four of our horses during the evening.
I sent Pryor to investigate.
He searched for three days,
finding only a remnant of a robe and an old moccasin,
which Sacagawea felt belonged to Crow warriors.
Pryor believed that our horses had been driven down the river rapidly.
Adding to our misery, we soon learned
that wolves and dogs had stolen most of our dried meat.

We came upon an extraordinary rock formation
on the south side of the Yellowstone.

The projection rose to a height of at least two hundred feet.
One side was so steep, it could not be climbed,
but the other side was less challenging,
and I was determined to scale it.
I discovered there a number of Indian carvings.
I added my own inscription with my name and the date.
At the very top, I was rewarded
with a most majestic view in all directions.
I named the formation "Pompy's Pillar" in honor of Jean Baptiste,
the youngest and most delightful member of our delegation.

We reached the junction of the Yellowstone and Missouri on August 2.
There we planned to rest and hunt
and amuse ourselves until Lewis caught up to us.
Unfortunately, the mosquitoes also thought this a good resting place,
and they arrived in swarms.
No one could sleep for they made their way into our tents.
We couldn't hunt because they jammed our barrels;
we couldn't dress skins or dry meat;
we had no choice but to move on.
I wrote a note for Lewis and stuck it on a pole at the river junction.
We packed and moved downriver,
where we were finally relieved
when a cold wind arrived, sweeping the pests away.

On August 12, we were overjoyed to sight Captain Lewis's boat.
Delight quickly turned to alarm when we did not see Lewis in it.
Relief followed when we learned he was lying in the bottom of the canoe.
He had suffered a gunshot wound to the thigh
just the day before and was in much pain.
Cruzatte, who is blind in one eye and does not see well with the other,
had mistaken him for an elk.
Although it was an agonizing situation all the way around,
I found the predicament easier to deal with
than if Lewis had been shot by an Indian,
an occurrence that would have required military action.

Examining Lewis's injury, I noted it was a very grave wound.
The ball had passed through his left thigh
and made a three-inch cut across his right buttock.
Lewis was in much agony.

As we exchanged information about our travels,
we learned of a graver circumstance
arising from Lewis's party's encounters with the Indians.
The entire incident was largely the fault of the Field brothers,
who had fallen asleep on duty and had their guns stolen.
Drouillard woke up at the first light of dawn
to see an Indian stealing his gun also.
A struggle for ownership ensued.
Lewis, meanwhile, reached for his rifle, but it, too, was gone.
He quickly drew his pistol and rushed outside
to see a second Indian running off with his rifle.
He signaled to him to lay it down or be shot.
The Indian chose to honor the command.

Drouillard managed to seize back his gun,
while both Field brothers pursued
the Indian who had stolen their rifles.
They caught him and wrestled the rifles out of his hands,
but in the scuffle, Reubin Field plunged a knife into the warrior's heart.
The wounded brave drew one final breath then fell dead.
In the meantime, Lewis witnessed more Indians
attempting to drive off their horses.
Lewis called out an order to pursue and shoot the Indians.
When one of the Indians turned a British musket on Lewis,
Lewis brought his rifle to his shoulder, aimed, and fired.
The shot went through the warrior's belly.
The Blackfoot fell but then raised himself up and returned fire.
Lewis said he felt the wind of the bullet over his head.
Unable to reload, Lewis quickly retreated.
Back at camp, the men burned the evidence of the Indians' visit—
four shields, two bows, two quivers of arrows.

Lewis placed a medal around the neck of the dead Indian
so those who followed would know
we were not the kind of men to be taken advantage of.

Taking stock of the situation, Lewis knew
they had to quickly get out of that territory,
for they were a party of four whites deep in Blackfoot terrain
and could expect revenge at any moment.
They retreated on horseback, covering eight miles per hour.
Luckily the roads were good.
They took a break about three o'clock and allowed the horses to graze,
calculating that they had covered sixty-three miles.
They remounted and covered another seventeen miles by dark,
arriving on a flat plain where they killed and ate a buffalo
before they resumed their journey.
Thunderclouds rolled overhead and lightning split the sky.
They passed a large herd of buffalo.
At two in the morning, Lewis ordered a halt,
bringing to a close their hundred-mile ride.
They rested for several hours,
but at dawn, they soldiered on.
Finally, they rejoined the rest of Lewis's party.
Lewis noted then how ragged their clothes had become,
for they were nearly naked.
Of course, no one had time to take make new clothes.

Despite his pain and need of recovery,
Lewis insisted that we resume our travels,
so we left the following day.
The air was cool, and the mosquitoes no longer troubled us.
It was only a journey of several days,
and then we arrived back in the Mandan-Hidatsa grand village.
A large crowd of people gathered to watch us disembark.
We saluted them several times with blasts from our blunderbuss.

Our old friends the Mandan chiefs, Black Cat and Big White,
and also One Eye of the Hidatsa, were the first to greet us.
We engaged in hugs, small presents, and smoking ceremonies.
Great numbers of Indians visited us at our camp—
some to renew our friendship,
others seeking to exchange robes and skins.
We were presented with bushels of corn from four of the villages.
One gift of corn was so large that our canoe could not hold it.

Much of the formal smoking and negotiations were left to me,
as Captain Lewis was still weak and in pain.
We learned disappointing news in our meetings with the chiefs.
Our mission of promoting peace among the tribes had failed.
The Arikaras and the Mandans were warring.
The Hidatsas were raiding Shoshone camps in the Rockies again.
They had killed Shoshone tribesmen,
possibly men from Cameahwait's band.
Sioux warriors had recently attacked the Mandans.

We felt further discouraged when our invitation to the various chiefs
to travel with us to Washington was turned down.
Black Cat would like to go, but he feared the Sioux.
I promised protection, many presents,
and the building of an American trading post,
but still the answer was "no."
Big White did agree to come,
but he insisted that his wife and son
and Jessaume, the trader, be allowed to go also,
along with Jessaume's Indian wife and two sons.
We feared this would overload the canoes,
but we agreed, desperate to bring chiefs to Washington.

I encouraged Charbonneau and Sacagawea to return with us also.
I could find Charbonneau employment and land,
but Charbonneau stated that he knew no person in the United States,
and he knew no way of earning a living there.

I reluctantly acceded to his wishes and paid him a sum of $500.33.
As I did so, I thought of the services provided by Sacagawea.
She had been by far the more useful of the pair,
but we could offer her nothing.

As our departure time neared,
I found myself nearly desperate with desire
to remain connected with this family.
Charbonneau was disagreeable enough,
but I had learned to deal with his arrogant personality,
and I even held a measure of affection for him.
The thought of parting from Sacagawea and the beautiful child
was a pain I could hardly bear.

I offered to take their little son with me.
He was a beautiful and promising child.
I could give him a fine education
and would treat him as a son.
He would always be honored and well treated in my home.

But Sacagawea quickly let me know that this could not be so.
The child was not yet weaned.
Charbonneau added that they would consider sending the child
when he was older, if I were still agreeable then.

On August 16, we decided that our swivel gun was no longer of use to us.
We made a present of it, giving it to One Eye, the chief of the Hidatsa,
in hopes that it would ingratiate him to our causes.
We collected the chiefs in a circle,
where I addressed them with great ceremony.
I presented the swivel to One Eye,
charging him to remember the promises
of his Great White Father when he fired this gun.
He appeared to be much pleased.

We left the Hidatsa village then
and proceeded to the Mandan village of Chief Big White.
Many of the Mandan chiefs and large numbers of his friends
had gathered there to bid him a fond farewell.
The men sat in a circle smoking.
The women stood and cried loudly
to show their grief at Big White's departure.

Finally, the chief, his wife, and son boarded.
They were followed by Jessaume and Jessaume's wife and children.
All of the people wept, united in their tribute to their beloved chief.
Perhaps they feared he would not return.
We proceeded with a final salute from our gun.

PART 8—THE YEARS THAT FOLLOWED

1806–1812
NORTH DAKOTA TO MISSOURI TO NORTH DAKOTA

SACAGAWEA

While we enjoyed our life in the Hidatsa village,
Captain Clark sent letters describing his own life in St. Louis,
where he hunted and fished
and raised crops and children with his new wife.
Always he urged us to keep our promise
to bring him our son.

I wished desperately to visit my Shoshone people,
but I knew travel westward would be difficult.
Despite the Captains' urgings that we all live in peace,
the years that followed were years of war.
The Sioux and Blackfeet fought against the Mandan and Hidatsa.
The white settlers and traders pushed west,
but the native peoples struck against them.
A journey to Shoshone land would be a perilous journey.

After three years had passed, however,
Charbonneau became restless to travel in a new direction.
He said he was tired of the hard life of trapping and hunting.

Perhaps the white man's life would be an easier life.
We packed our belongings and traveled to Captain Clark's town.

We saw immediately that St. Louis was a large village
with many lodges and many places of business.
In one store, we bought bread in the shape of a long loaf.
Charbonneau rested at a tavern,
where he drank a glass of whiskey
while Baptiste and I waited outside.
The blacksmith of this village had a special shop
for working on horseshoes and other metal.
We walked to the edge of the town to see
the brick buildings where men took their corn to be ground.
The people of the village lived in square houses of wood.
They traveled muddy roads to visit with friends.
We saw trading posts along the river.
They would provide a fine market for Charbonneau's furs.
There also we could buy many goods—
flour, iron cooking pots, cloth to make clothes.

We traveled to Captain Clark's home,
but he was not there.
His friends told us he had journeyed
to the home of the Great White Chief—President Jefferson.
Captain Clark's good friend, Auguste Chouteau,
provided us with lodging.

Charbonneau was anxious that Baptiste be baptized.
He made arrangements with the holy men who wore black robes.
We took Baptiste to their sacred lodge,
where a cross rose from a tall, pointed roof.
The priest uttered special words
and sprinkled water on Baptiste's forehead.

When Captain Clark returned,
he helped Charbonneau to buy land to farm.

We planted crops and raised hogs for meat.
Every Sunday we went to the holy lodge.
Kind women from the church gave me dresses of cloth
and showed me how to bundle my hair.
I learned to wash our clothes in kettles of hot water.

But after winter had passed and spring had turned to summer,
Charbonneau and I agreed that we were not happy.
This life of farming was not the life we wished to live.
I myself did not feel well.
The sharp pains in my stomach were always present.
I felt sure I would be well if only I could eat the roots
and the roasted game found in my village.
I longed to be with my people again,
especially my Shoshone family.
I thought often of my sister's son, whom I had adopted.
I wanted him to live with us.
Charbonneau longed for our old life also.
He signed papers with a fur trading expedition,
and Captain Clark gave us money for our land.

But Captain Clark desperately urged us to leave Baptiste.
Traveling would be dangerous for him, he warned,
for the Indians were now constantly warring with each other
as well as with the white men who invaded their territory.
Such a life would not be good for Baptiste.
In St. Louis, however, Baptiste would grow strong and tall.
During the day he would learn from the white man's books,
and every evening he would have plenty of food
and always a warm bed and a strong roof over his head.
We could come to visit with him every summer
and see for ourselves how he prospered.
His words were true words, I judged.
Captain Clark loved my child.
Perhaps he loved him more than Charbonneau did.
I knew that he would be a good father to him in our absence,

so I agreed, at least for this year, to honor Captain Clark's request.
I kissed my Baptiste goodbye with the promise that I would return
after I had visited with my people again.

We traveled with Manuel Lisa's trading expedition.
We were always alert for attacks,
but we arrived safely in the Mandan-Hidatsa villages in early summer.
Although I still did not feel well, it felt good to be in our old home.
We decided to rest there through the winter.
Charbonneau promised we would push on
and travel to my Shoshone homeland in the spring.
When the rivers thawed, we set out on our journey,
but we had not traveled far when we met other traders
who told us we could not safely travel
to the camping grounds of the Three Forks.
The Blackfeet warriors were angry and fierce and continually raiding.
We were forced to change direction
and to travel to a safe place to build a new fort.
The new fort was called Manuel Lisa
in honor of the headman of the expedition.

In August, I gave birth to my daughter Lisette.
Ah, how I wished that Baptiste could see his sister!
He would have been eager to teach her many things.
And how I wished we could travel back to him,
for we found that Fort Manuel was not a safe place either.
The trappers and traders argued amongst themselves,
and the surrounding tribes were at war with one another.

I did my best to care for my child.
She was a fine, healthy baby,
but it was not easy for me.
The old pains and ill feelings persisted.
When the winter months were upon us again,
Charbonneau had to make good use of what time was left for hunting,
so he spent many hours away from my bed.

My head burned with fire,
while my hands were cold like ice.
I could not eat or nurse my child;
I trembled under my blanket.
I remembered past days when Captain Lewis and Captain Clark
stayed by my side, administering poultices and drops of medicine.
But there was no one in this fort who could do that.
Besides, all of the men were in danger themselves.
Nearly every day they would return from the hunt with more bad news.
They were often stalked and threatened by angry braves.
One day they returned to tell us that three of our men
had been killed by warriors from a local tribe.

So I wrapped my arms around my daughter Lisette
and my thoughts around my son Baptiste.
I consoled myself with the knowledge
that all would be well when spring arrived.
My fever would then be lifted,
and the native peoples would be content to turn their thoughts
to tasks of gathering food and shooting game,
and we could travel to my Shoshone home.
We would spend the summer there,
and when the leaves began to fall,
we would repack our belongings.
Charbonneau and I would then take Lisette to St. Louis,
to the home of Captain Clark.
There we would be reunited with our beloved Jean Baptiste.

1806–1812
NORTH DAKOTA TO MISSOURI

CLARK

Over the next few days, I found myself longing intensely
for Charbonneau's family.
I was desperate in my need to be reassured
that we would be reunited again.
Hence, I wrote a letter to Charbonneau,
informing him of my concerns.

I began by telling him I wished I had had more time to talk with him
and to be more persuasive with my entreaty
that he and his family come to St. Louis with me.
I recalled that we had been a long time together.
He had conducted himself in such a manner as to gain my friendship.
I acknowledged that Sacagawea had deserved
a greater reward for her contributions
than we were capable of providing her with at the time.
Finally, I reminded him of my fondness for his son Baptiste.
I renewed my pledge to take him and raise him as my own child,
promising to educate and treat him as a son.
Also, I laid out the various plans whereby he, Charbonneau,

might be inclined to come and live near me in St. Louis.
I could furnish him with farmland and hogs and cows.

If he wished to visit his family in Montreal,
I would serve as caretaker of his family until he returned.
If he wished to hold a position as interpreter,
I could arrange a post for him.
If he wished to come as a merchandiser,
I would help him to sell his wares
and even become a partner to his enterprise.
I advised him to collect as many furs, pelts, and skins as he could
and bring them down to St. Louis by spring.
He, of course, would also bring Sacagawea and Baptiste.
I gave him instructions to make contact with the Governor's house
for accommodations in case of my absence,
and I urged him to write me, to relieve my anxiety,
to let me know of his plans.
I closed it by saying that I wished his family great success,
and I waited with anxious expectation
to see again my little dancing boy, Baptiste.
I vowed I would remain forever his friend.
I sent the letter by canoe with a trusted trader
and hoped that it would soon be in Charbonneau's possession.

Over the next few days,
I had the opportunity to reflect on the fine service and fellowship
Lewis and I had enjoyed with our men.
Our band of explorers had molded well
and had become the most hardy, resourceful,
well-disciplined, trustworthy, and loyal troop of men.
Patrick Gass showed himself a master craftsman
in the building of forts and canoes.
John Colter proved one of our most daring men
as well our finest hunter.
Pierre Cruzatte and George Drouillard had the knowledge
of the native languages that we so often needed.

Drouillard was a fine boatman as well,
and we counted him with our best hunters and scouts.
The Field brothers, Joseph and Reubin,
were excellent woodsmen and hunters
and were the first called upon for advanced scouting.
William Bratton had been our master blacksmith,
lending his skills both to us and to the various tribes.
Every man who completed the journey put their trust in our leadership,
even when they disagreed with our decisions.
Their supreme loyalty carried us to the Pacific and back.

I would never forget the friendships forged with various Indian leaders.
Big White and Black Cat of the Mandans had given us wise counsel.
Cameahwait, Sacagawea's Shoshone brother,
had provided valuable information about the navigable rivers
and mountain passes we would cross on our passage to the Pacific.
He had accorded me the highest gift any man could give—his very name.
Chief Twisted Hair, Old Toby and his sons,
Chief Yellept of the Walla Wallas—
we counted them in the ranks of our most trusted and valued friends.

As far as the relationship that Captain Lewis and I maintained,
it was a marvel to think about how well we had jointly worked
to lead this group of men on such an arduous and lengthy mission.
What had begun as mutual admiration
had increased and strengthened with each trial and triumph.
At no time did we ever disagree or even come close to conflict.
His introspective nature was appreciated by the men
and formed the balance needed for my more gregarious personality.

The land we had crossed and the wildlife we had encountered—
they were surely a trial at times,
but they were always a source of beauty and wonder—
the plains with the buffalo, the prairie dog,
the wolves, the big sheep, the antelope;
the cliffs along the twists and turns of the rivers;

the snow-peaked mountains that loomed before us;
the sandy shores where we became acquainted
with the great whale and the sea otters;
and the Pacific Ocean, which we judged had been unduly named,
for with the huge, crashing waves and roaring surf,
it was surely the most unpeaceful of waters.

Giving thought to the goals President Jefferson had set before us,
I realized with great satisfaction that they had all been met
to the best of our ability.
We had traveled the continent and reached the Pacific.
Although we had not discovered a Northwest Passage,
we had learned that none existed.
We had established good relations with many Indian tribes
and had acquired useful knowledge
of the geography, the terrain, and the waterways.

It had been a remarkable journey,
but with each passing day on the river,
our thoughts began to travel in a forward direction.
We were anxious to know what events had occurred in our absence,
and we longed for news of our families and countrymen.
We were encouraged in early September
when we began to meet small detachments
of white men coming up the river from the East.
On September 3, we met with a trading party.
Mr. James Aird, a Scotsman from Prairie du Chien,
greeted us warmly and apprised us
of what had transpired with regard to our nation.
We were heartened to learn
that President Jefferson was well and had been reelected.
General Wilkins, governor of the Louisiana Territory,
had engaged in skirmishes with Spanish and British ships.
Two Indians had been hanged in St. Louis for murder.
Aaron Burr and Alexander Hamilton had fought a duel.
We could scarcely believe the outcome—Hamilton was dead.

We were saddened to learn of a fire in the home of our good friend,
Jean Pierre Chouteau, in St. Louis.
His residence had burned to the ground.

Several days after talking with Mr. Aird,
we met up with Robert McClellan, a former scout with the army.
He informed us that the people in the United States
had long ago given up on us.
They had heard various stories—
that we had been killed by Indians
or that the Spaniards had enslaved us in their mines.

On September 20, we knew ourselves to be back in civilized country
when we saw cows grazing along the bank.
We erupted with shouts of joy.
We put our boats in at the village of La Charette.
The men fired a salute, which was answered
by three rounds from five trading boats on the riverbank.
The citizens rushed to greet us.
French and Americans alike expressed
great relief and pleasure at our return,
for they had all feared that we were long ago dead.

The following day we arrived in St. Charles.
Being a Sunday, a number of ladies and gentlemen
were walking on the bank.
We saluted the village with three rounds from our blunderbuss
then docked in the lower part of town.
A great number of villagers greeted us.
We were moved by their polite, polished manners and their hospitality.
At Fort Belle Fontaine, we received a similar welcome.
We took Big White and his family to the supply store
and furnished them with clothes.

On September 23, we descended the Mississippi and rounded to St. Louis.
The shore was lined with people welcoming us home.

I was told that they numbered no less than five thousand,
all of them issuing their heartiest thanks and relief
that we had arrived safely on the Missouri shore.
We rejoiced much that evening among dignitaries and friends
and retired, looking forward to traveling on to our family homes.
It would be good to see our parents.
We had been gone so long from them.

Departing St. Louis, I proceeded to Louisville, Kentucky,
where I visited with my parents and other family members.
From there I proceeded to Virginia
with the intention of courting Julia Hancock
and persuading her to be my wife.
She had been on my mind throughout the expedition.
Indeed, I had named a river in the high country for her.
My wishes were fulfilled.
We were married and established our residence in St. Louis,
where we received an array of visitors,
always anxious to view my museum of frontier curiosities
and hear my tales of our travels.

Much to my consternation,
York, my slave and constant companion,
made appeals for his own freedom upon our return.
He wished to rejoin his wife in Kentucky.
At first, I was determined that he would remain with me,
but I was finally persuaded by the arguments of my own wife.
After attaining his free status, York reunited with his wife
and did freighting business in Kentucky and Tennessee.

In 1807, President Jefferson accorded me the title
of Brigadier General of the Militia in the Louisiana Territory.
I later became the official United States Agent of Indian Affairs
when Missouri was declared a territory.

For some years, I endeavored to stay abreast
of those dear comrades of the Corps of Discovery,
but the separation of time and distance made it more and more difficult.
My cherished friend, Meriwether Lewis,
died of a self-inflicted gunshot wound on October 12, 1806.
I was grief-stricken by his death.
I attributed his suicide to the spells of melancholy he was subject to
and the difficulties associated with adjusting to a new and ordered life.
In honor of our friendship, I named my firstborn son for him.

I was to hear little from Sacagawea and Charbonneau
for the next several years after our return.
The information I did receive from various traders and officials
was that travel was indeed very dangerous
because of the threats presented by warring tribes.

So I was heartily gladdened in the fall of 1809
when Charbonneau presented himself
and his family to me in St. Louis.
He and Sacagawea expressed a desire
to take up residence on Missouri lands.
I accordingly assisted in the purchase of farmland
and small herds of pigs and cows.
But in the months that followed,
I observed how their enthusiasm waned,
and I knew that they would not be content to remain confined here.
Sacagawea, especially, was pining to revisit her Shoshone people
and to see about the welfare of the adopted son she had left with relatives.
So I agreed to buy their land and animals,
and they agreed to leave Jean Baptiste in my care
while they traveled off again to Indian lands.
Sacagawea vowed that she would return
when her mission was accomplished
so that she might be again with her young son.

It was not to be so, however.
Because of the persistent tribal warfare
and the increasing hostile actions of the Blackfeet,
Charbonneau's trading expedition was unable
to reach the Shoshone villages.
The traders were forced to venture on to Fort Manuel some distance away.
Skirmishes occurred near Fort Manuel on a regular basis,
and living conditions were precarious.
Nearly a year after their departure,
I received a report from John Luttig, the appointed clerk reporter,
informing me that the wife of Charbonneau had died of a putrid fever.
The clerk described her as "good" and "the best woman in the fort."
He added that she left behind a fine infant girl, Lisette.

I could scarcely believe the news!
Sacagawea had been ill several times during our journey,
but she always recovered with increased zest and heartiness.
I found I could not put the letter or the news aside.
I read and reread the words over the next few weeks,
searching for more meaning and understanding.
The buffalo robe that Sacagawea
had presented to me at our first meeting—
I retrieved it from the bundled items in our storage shed
and placed it at the foot of my bed.

Rumors abounded for some time afterward
that Charbonneau had been killed during a raid on the fort.
The baby, Lisette, survived and was brought
to my home in St. Louis by John Luttig himself.
I completed the proper paperwork then
and became the formal guardian of both Jean Baptiste and Lisette.

So I was astounded several years later
when I opened my front door
and there stood Charbonneau himself,
his hair considerably grayed, his shoulders stooped.

Remarkably, he had survived the raid
and had made his way to friendly camps.
He was a frequent visitor in St. Louis from that time on,
trading his furs at the markets in the city
and visiting with me and the children when he felt so inclined.
Jean Baptiste was the best of pupils.
He was educated first at the Baptist school near our home
and later at the St. Louis Academy,
attending classes alongside my own sons.

My thoughts have often dwelled on our dearest Sacagawea.
She had been such a hearty girl
with a spirit and generosity that remain unmatched.
I have wondered what I could have done
to have persuaded her to remain in St. Louis,
and yet, I know that such a life would not have brought her happiness.
I can only hope that she looks down from her heavenly home
and sees how well her son Baptiste has fared,
for he is still a dancing lad with all of the grace and spirit of his mother,
and he is a bright child who profits well from his schooling.
He has been both a fine son to me
and a fine companion to those about him.

SOURCES

Books

Ambrose, Stephen E. *Undaunted Courage: Meriwether Lewis, Thomas Jefferson, and the Opening of the American West.* New York: Simon and Schuster, 1996.

Berne, Emma Carlson. *Sacagawea: Crossing the Continent with Lewis and Clark.* New York: Sterling, 2010.

Blakeless, John, ed. *The Journals of Lewis and Clark.* New York: Penguin, 1964.

Brooks, Noah. *First Across the Continent: The Story of the Exploring Expedition of Lewis and Clark in 1804-5-6.* A public domain book–free on the web.

Clark, Ella and Edmonds, Margot. *Sacagawea of the Lewis and Clark Expedition.* Berkeley: University of California Press, 1979.

Edwards, Judith. *Lewis and Clark's Journey of Discovery in American History.* Berkeley Heights: Enslow, 1999.

Hebard, Grace. *Sacagawea: Guide and Interpreter of Lewis and Clark.* Mineola: Dover, 2002.

Hill, William. *Following Lewis and Clark's Track: The Story of the Corps of Discovery.* Independence: Oregon-California Trails Association, 2001.

Howard, Harold. *Sacagawea.* Norman: University of Oklahoma Press, 1971.

Moeller, Bill and Jan. *Lewis and Clark: A Photographic Journey.* Missoula: Mountain Press, 1999.

Moulton, Gary, ed. *The Lewis and Clark Journals: An American Epic of Discovery.* Lincoln: University of Nebraska Press, 2003.

Websites

Butterfield, Bonnie. *Sacagawea: From Captive to Expedition Interpreter to Legend.* www.bonniebutterfield.com/NativeAmericans.html, 2010.

Hunter, Frances. *Frances Hunter's American Heroes Blog.* https://franceshunter.wordpress.com, various posts on Lewis and Clark Expedition, 2010-2012.

Films

Burns, Ken, film maker. *Lewis and Clark: The Journey of the Corps of Discovery.* https://www.pbs.org/lewisandclark/, 1997.

Map

"File:Carte Lewis-Clark Expedition-fr.svg." Wikimedia Commons, the free media repository. 29 Jan 2015, 23:32 UTC. 10 Oct 2019, 03:47 <https://commons.wikimedia.org/w/index.php?title=File:Carte_Lewis-Clark_Expedition-fr.svg&oldid=148376716> text translated to English by author

ABOUT THE AUTHOR

Charlotte Ellington resides in St. Albans, Missouri, near the very spot where Captain Meriwether Lewis scaled a cliff and nearly fell to his death in the very early days of the Expedition. Her early fascination with the Lewis and Clark Expedition began years ago when she visited the Museum of Westward Expansion located beneath St. Louis' iconic Arch. The walk-through exhibit featured colorful murals with inspirational quotes from the diaries of Lewis and Clark as well as recreated scenes with life-sized stuffed animals. Of course, Sacagawea played a crucial role in the narrative, and Charlotte has always had an interest in noteworthy Native American women. Her first two books, *Beloved Mother: The Story of Nancy Ward* and *Dancing Leaf,* portray strong Cherokee women.

In addition to reading and writing, Charlotte enjoys spending time with family, which includes her husband, two sons, two daughters-in-law, and four grandchildren.